"We have unfinished business."

The only unfinished business she was aware they had was the time she had spent in his arms—and she certainly had no intention of finishing that! "I don't think so." Joy shook her head. What did Marcus Ballantyne think she was? Did he really believe she was a woman who had a string of lovers? And did he want to be one of them?

"I want you, Joy." Marcus spoke almost angrily. "I've tried to put you out of my mind, but it just isn't possible. I want you. And I intend to have you. Exclusively," he added grimly.

Joy stared up at him. He didn't want to be *one* of her lovers, he wanted to be *the* one—and the *only* one!

CAROLE MORTIMER is the youngest of three children and grew up in a small English village with her parents and two brothers. She still loves nothing better than going "home" to visit her family. She has three very active sons, four cats, and a dog, which doesn't leave her a lot of time for hobbies! She has written almost one hundred romance novels for Harlequin.

Books by Carole Mortimer

CAROLE MORTIMER

The One and Only

Harlequin Books

TORONTO • NEW YORK • LONDON
AMSTERDAM • PARIS • SYDNEY • HAMBURG
STOCKHOLM • ATHENS • TOKYO • MILAN
MADRID • WARSAW • BUDAPEST • AUCKLAND

Peter—
Eternity

ISBN 0-373-11793-0

THE ONE AND ONLY

First North American Publication 1996.

CHAPTER ONE

WHAT a bore!

God, how had she ever got herself into this? She hadn't—Casey had got her into it. As usual. It was typical of Casey: he had been getting her into one scrape or another all their lives.

But this time he had excelled himself.

It had all sounded so simple when he had explained it to her a couple of weeks ago. She should have known then—nothing was ever simple where Casey was concerned.

First prize in a Valentine competition. A week's stay in a luxurious hotel, plus a show and supper on Valentine's night with a television star.

'It sounds marvellous, Casey,' Joy had told him distractedly when he called round for dinner with her one evening.

'Bad day at the library?' Casey had quirked curious brows at her, blue eyes alight with mischief. Again, as usual.

How could anyone have a 'bad day' working in a library? And yet, as Casey very well knew, too many of Joy's working days were fraught with tension. Still, beggars couldn't be choosers—and she needed the job. Even with all its problems.

Her grimace in Casey's direction, as he had leant so casually against one of the kitchen units as he watched her prepare their meal, had told its own story.

'You should have left months ago—sorry.' Casey had held his hands up apologetically as Joy glared up at him warningly. 'I know I promised after—well, after, that I wouldn't say I told you so——'

'And you've done nothing *but* since!' she had snapped, her eyes sparkling deeply green.

'Only because you will insist on sticking it out there, putting yourself through unnecessary grief, wasting your love on someone who... Well, this competition is just what you need to cheer you up.' He had hastily changed the subject as he saw the light of battle in Joy's eyes.

At five feet two she might be a foot shorter than he was, but he knew that, if he pushed too much, the temper that matched her red hair would surely surface. It might take time, but it did surface.

'Cheer me up?' She frowned as she realised what he had said. 'What does it have to do with me?'

'Well, I can hardly go on this week's holiday, to the show and then supper, so I naturally thought you might like to go instead of me. And——'

'Just stop there, Casey,' Joy interrupted drily, abandoning the dinner for a moment, sensing that she needed to give the whole of her attention to what Casey was saying—otherwise she could, as she had many times in the past, find herself in a situation she would rather not be in.

The two of them were cousins but, because both sets of their parents had been working, they had spent most school holidays together, staying at their mutual grandparents' house, and had grown up more like brother and sister. And Joy had spent most of that time getting Casey out of the scrapes he had managed to get himself into, or ones he had embroiled her in. Life without Casey, she had decided long ago, would be a lot lonelier, but it would also be a lot more trouble-free. And she sensed one of Casey's impending scrapes . . .!

'Why can't you go on the holiday, Casey?' She looked at him searchingly, not fooled for a moment by the innocent expression on his boyishly handsome face. With his dark curly hair, laughing blue eyes and rakishly handsome face, Casey had a look of uncomplicated innocence—but Joy knew, from experience, that it was just a look. 'And to the show and supper afterwards? I would have thought it would have been just up your street to go and wallow in the lap of luxury, to go out for the evening with some beautifully ravishing television star, on Valentine's night, of all nights. You——'

'The television star is Danny Eames, Joy,' Casey cut in drily.

'Danny Eames?' she repeated frowningly. 'But Danny Eames is a——'

'Man,' her cousin finished impatiently. 'Of course he's a man!'

A rather attractive one too, as Joy recalled. He was the actor appearing regularly in a popular detective programme on Friday evenings. 'How on earth did you manage to win an evening out with a man?' Joy decided she had either missed something in the earlier conversation, or Casey was keeping something back. And, knowing Casey as she did, she thought she knew which one it was!

He looked more than a little irritated now. 'Well, if you must know . . .'

'Oh, I think I must.' She nodded derisively.

'I entered a competition in one of those women's magazines Lisa is always reading. And I won the damned thing!' he added disgustedly.

Lisa was Casey's steady girlfriend of the last year, if the word 'steady' could be applied to the stormy relationship they both seemed to enjoy.

'I told her the damned things were all a con, that no one ever actually won anything in them,' Casey continued disgruntledly as Joy stared at him.

'And then you won.' Joy's lips twiched as she made an effort to hold back her humour. 'First prize!'

'Yes!' he bit out impatiently. 'And the people who ran the competition assumed Casey Simms was a woman——'

'Well, they would—when the prize was Valentine's night out with a handsome hunk!' Joy knew she wasn't going to be able to contain her laughter much longer—the humour of the situation was just too much.

He glared at her. 'Don't rub it in!'

She chewed on her top lip to stop the throaty laughter from erupting. 'And just where are you and Danny supposed to be having this intimate dinner for two?' Casey had really done it this time. But then, he had never done anything by halves.

'In London,' he snapped. 'But we aren't—*you* and he are!' Casey looked at her challengingly.

She shook her head, repressed laughter making her eyes appear an even deeper green than usual. 'I don't think so.'

'I can't go!' her cousin wailed.

'Well, obviously not,' Joy conceded, openly smiling now. 'But Lisa could——'

'No way!' Casey instantly protested. 'Do you think I'm stupid enough to let my girlfriend go out for the evening, especially that evening, with a lech like Danny Eames is reputed to be?'

Joy raised auburn brows, brows much darker than the long fiery-coloured hair she wore confined when at work, but preferred to leave loose about her shoulders at other times. 'But it's all right to send your favourite cousin out for the evening with him?' she derided drily.

'My *only* cousin,' he corrected distractedly. 'And my favourite one, of course,' he added at her openly mocking expression. 'I'm going to look so stupid if it ever comes out that I entered a competition in a women's magazine——'

'Maybe you should have thought of that earlier,' she pointed out reasonably.

'Joy, you know I would do the same for you if the positions were reversed,' he persisted wheedlingly.

'The answer is no, Casey,' she told him dismissively.

'Oh, please, Joy.' He looked at her pleadingly.

Joy knew that look only too well—and the trouble it could get her into. 'I said no, Casey,' she repeated firmly.

Which was why she was here now, pretending to be Casey Simms for the week!

The hotel was as luxurious as Casey had promised it would be, and she had enjoyed the little she had seen of London since her arrival yesterday. But Danny Eames, far from being the interesting individual Casey had persuaded her he would be, was one of the most boring people, male or female, she had ever met in her life!

Lisa had lent her a dress to wear for the evening; in fact, Lisa had provided most of the clothes Joy had brought with her, after looking through Joy's wardrobe and declaring its contents were much too librarianish. Joy's protests of that being exactly what she was had been met with little sympathy, let alone understanding. And with Casey as well as Lisa to argue against, each of them as incorrigible as the other, Joy hadn't stood a chance, and had arrived at the hotel yesterday with two suitcases full of Lisa's expensively flamboyant clothing. As a model, Lisa often managed to buy her clothes cheaper than she might otherwise have done, and she usually chose the clothes that would most get her noticed.

As with the dress Joy was wearing this evening. It was unlike anything she had ever worn, or dreamt of wearing, in her life before. She had to admit that the green shimmering material made her eyes appear even deeper in colour, and her hair glowed fiery-red as it fell loosely to just below her shoulders. But the dress also clung to the slender length of her body, finishing abruptly several inches above her shapely knees. But of the evening gowns Lisa had provided, this was the least revealing—the black one was backless, and the red one virtually frontless!

But she needn't have worried about the allure of the dress; Danny Eames was far too interested in himself to notice what Joy was or wasn't wearing. She also had the feeling that he might have enjoyed the company of the real Casey Simms more than hers.

As it was, he hadn't stopped talking about himself since the representative of the magazine had introduced the two of them earlier this evening in the foyer of Joy's hotel. The only time he had given his ego a rest was when they were actually watching the show, and even then he had wasted little time, after they had left their seats during the interval, before beginning to criticise the actors in the show, at the same time making it plain he could do a better job of all the parts, male and female, than his fellow actors and actresses were doing.

And supper after the show, for all it was in one of the most famous restaurants in London—Joy recognised several of the diners as actors, or faces she had seen in the daily newspapers—was turning out to be just as much of a nightmare.

Joy was going to strangle Casey when she got home at the weekend. This had to be the longest evening of her life!

And what made it worse was that several of the other women dining here were actually eyeing her enviously for her companion of the evening; as far as Joy was concerned, any one of them was welcome to the egotistical idiot!

'... and so I told the director that if that was all he wanted to go and hire himself a performing monkey...'

Joy faded in, and as quickly faded out again of the one-sided conversation at their table, deciding as she did so that the director had probably known when he was talking to Danny Eames that he *had* hired a performing monkey. Although a monkey would probably have had more intelligence than Danny Eames seemed to have. Joy pitied any woman who had to spend more than one evening in this man's company. Thank God she wasn't one of them. He——

'. . . to introduce me to your dining companion, Danny?'

Joy had been in danger of falling asleep with her eyes open, but the different timbre of voice, this one huskily deep, broke her out of her inner torment, and she turned curiously in the direction of that voice. Any diversion had to be welcome.

And this wasn't just 'any diversion', she quickly realised, instantly recognising the man who now stood so confidently beside their table as the man who played the part of Danny's boss in the detective programme: Marcus Ballantyne.

This man was actually the real star of the television series Danny Eames seemed to feel would fall apart without the aid of his so-brilliant acting. And Joy should know—she had been listening to just how wonderful Danny thought he was for the last four hours.

But Marcus Ballantyne really was a true talent, star of numerous television series over the last fifteen years. He had made his big break into Hollywood ten years ago, returning there periodically to star in films that were inevitably box-office hits. But he remained true to his native England, preferring to make his home there, occasionally making appearances on the West End stage in plays destined to be a success simply because Marcus Ballantyne deemed them worthy of his time and talent.

But the last thing Joy needed was another ego-maniac to join them and bore her to sleep!

Joy knew Marcus Ballantyne was in his late thirties—older than Danny Eames by at least ten years. He was well over six feet tall, with slightly overlong dark hair, and deceptively sleepy blue eyes, a deep, dark blue that, as Joy looked up at him, she could see contained a sharp intelligence. Maybe she wasn't going to be bored, after all...

Danny had risen hurriedly to his feet at the sound of the other man's voice, some of that overbearing self-confidence leaving him as he shook the older man by the hand, evidence that even he bowed to the older man's superior talent. 'Marcus,' he greeted, a little too enthusiastically. 'I didn't know you came to places like this.' He looked pointedly around the noisy restaurant.

'I'm not in my dotage, Danny,' the other man drawled derisively.

The younger man's cheeks were slightly flushed. 'No, of course not. I just...well, I didn't think... It's good to see you, Marcus,' Danny finished lamely.

'Is it?' the older man drawled, dark brows raised mockingly.

Joy looked more intently at Marcus Ballantyne; he obviously shared her opinion that Danny was an idiot, and he made no attempt to hide his contempt for the younger man. Which posed the question: why had he bothered to come over to their table at all if he felt that way about Danny?

As he turned that probing blue gaze in her direction, Joy suddenly knew exactly why.

There was no mistaking the admiration in that gaze as it swept over her appraisingly. Joy felt a quiver of awareness down her spine as she seemed unable to break that searching blue gaze.

This had never happened to her before. She had never been instantly physically aware of a man in her life before. But there was something about the hard lines of Marcus Ballantyne's face that was mesmerising; the lean length of his body in the casually expensive clothes exuded a physical magnetism that Joy couldn't help being completely aware of.

She shifted uncomfortably as he continued to look at her. This was ridiculous! She wasn't some star-struck teenager, but a grown woman of twenty-seven, and certainly not the type to be impressed by a man whose face was famous enough for him to be recognised wherever he went. Hadn't she instantly recognised him herself, although she rarely watched television or went to the cinema?

She turned away abruptly as she realised how stupidly she was behaving, and looked at Danny instead. But even that was a mistake, because he just looked more young and affected than ever compared with the hard assurance of the other man.

'Introduce us, Danny,' Marcus Ballantyne instructed the younger man, his gaze not leaving Joy's slightly flushed face.

Danny looked more flustered than ever. 'Er—this is Casey Simms—er—Joy. She prefers to be called Joy,' he introduced awkwardly, his bravado completely gone in the face of the other man's quiet authority.

'Why?' Marcus Ballantyne addressed the question to Joy, totally ignoring the younger man now as he pulled out the chair beside her and sat down without being invited to do so.

Which brought him all the closer to her, and Joy could feel her hands shaking slightly as she clasped them together beneath the table. This man was something else, unlike anyone she had ever met before. No wonder he was so much in demand both on television and the big screen; he was magnetic. And Joy could feel herself being drawn unresistingly towards him. Unresisting because she simply couldn't break the spell of that steady gaze.

'Why Joy?' he repeated huskily, leaning forward slightly, effectively cutting Danny out of their conversation as the younger man resumed his seat opposite Joy.

She moistened lips that felt suddenly dry. 'Casey is... It's an old family name,' she told him truthfully, wondering if that slightly breathless voice could really be her own. But she knew it was, knew she had never felt such emotional confusion, knew her usual capable efficiency was deserting her. 'I prefer my other name—Joy.' She had refused point-blank to spend the whole evening with Danny Eames answering to her cousin's name, and had decided before meeting him that she would use her own name. He hadn't been concerned about her name anyway—in fact she was surprised he could even remember it to introduce her to the other man!

'So do I,' Marcus Ballantyne told her huskily. 'Much more...feminine.' His tone implied that that was exactly what he thought she was.

Joy swallowed hard, knowing she was—subtly—being flirted with. Ridiculous. She was a librarian from a small rural town in the south of England——

'And what do you do, Joy?' That cobalt-blue gaze continued to hold hers.

It was almost as if by doing so he had been able to read her thoughts. He obviously knew she wasn't an actress, otherwise their paths would probably have crossed before. But, somehow, just baldly stating that she worked in her local library didn't seem appropriate——

'Joy lives out of town.' Danny Eames was the one to answer the other man. 'She's an old... friend.'

She gave him a startled look at this explanation. What on earth...?

Marcus Ballantyne relaxed back in his chair now, watching her from beneath brooding brows. 'She doesn't look that old to me,' he finally drawled.

Danny gave a nervously dismissive laugh at the other man's obvious sarcasm. 'You know what I mean, Marcus.'

Joy knew what he was implying too—and she didn't like it one little bit! Why was Danny lying to the other man? What possible reason could he have for giving the impression that they had once been—even if they weren't now—involved?

'Yes,' the older man acknowledged gratingly, still looking at Joy. 'But that still doesn't tell me——'

'Marcus, I think your group of friends are trying to let you know they're leaving,' Danny cut in, looking pointedly over to the table where the other man had been sitting with a dozen or so people until a few minutes ago.

A rather attractive blonde, probably in her early twenties, was looking pointedly over at Marcus Ballantyne now as the rest of the group prepared to leave. Joy vaguely recognised her as an actress who had briefly appeared in a long-running soap, although the woman's name escaped her. Not that it was important what her name was; she was obviously expecting Marcus Ballantyne to rejoin them.

He studied Joy for several more long, lingering seconds before turning uninterestedly towards the other table, his mouth twisting with irritation as he saw the young blonde looking so longingly towards him. 'Excuse me for a few minutes.' He stood up in one fluid movement. 'But I'll be back,' he added, looking down at Joy again before turning to walk purposefully across the room to his friends.

Joy wasted no time, once he had gone, in turning accusingly to Danny. 'What do you think you're doing?' she demanded indignantly. 'I had never even met you before this evening!' And she never intended spending another evening in his company either. The things she did for Casey! The trouble was, her cousin would think the whole thing was hilarious. Ha ha!

Danny looked uncomfortable now, completely unlike the egotistical idiot he had been all evening. 'I'm really sorry about that, Joy,' he said sheepishly. 'I just... Well, I didn't want Marcus to know... Well...'

It was all suddenly clear to Joy: Danny didn't want the other man to know dinner with him had been first prize in a Valentine competition! It would be funny in any other circumstances, and if she hadn't just spent such an awful evening in his company. As it was——

'Please, Joy.' Danny put his hand cajolingly over hers. 'Not Marcus, of all people!'

She could understand why he didn't want the older man to know he had been a prize in a competition, and was sure Marcus Ballantyne would never have put himself in such a position. Obviously it had fed Danny's ego, but it wasn't something he wanted a man like Marcus Ballantyne to know about!

'I'll tell you what,' Danny continued encouragingly. 'I'll take you out to dinner tomorrow evening too if you'll just——'

'No! Er—no,' she refused, less desperately than her initial outburst. 'That really won't be necessary, Danny.' The mere thought of it was enough to send her into a panic. Another evening spent in this man's company? Never! Besides, if the truth were known, she didn't particularly want Marcus Ballantyne to think that she had entered a competition, obviously aimed at lovesick, impressionable women, to win an evening out with Danny Eames. 'I understand completely, Danny,' she soothed. 'And your secret is safe with me.' And her own!

'Thanks, Joy,' he said with obvious gratitude. 'I owe you one.'

'What secret?' drawled the familiar voice of Marcus Ballantyne as he resumed his seat next to Joy, looking at the two of them curiously with that compelling blue gaze.

Joy couldn't help her glance in the direction of his group of laughing friends as they prepared to leave, the pretty blonde in particular, who was still looking longingly in Marcus Ballantyne's direction as one of the other men in the group encouraged her to leave.

When Joy turned back, it was to find Marcus Ballantyne watching her with dark brows raised in questioning amusement. She could feel the heat in her cheeks at his mockery of her interest in his group of friends, expecially the young actress. Damn him!

'I hope we haven't dragged you away from your friends,' Joy told him stiltedly.

'Not in the least,' he dismissed easily, very relaxed in his chair, completely in command of the situation. 'I'm not interrupting anything, am I?' Again he looked at the two of them questioningly.

'Of course not,' Danny answered him a little too enthusiastically, obviously quite pleased that the other man had chosen to join them, but at the same time a little wary of his reasons for wanting to do so. 'I told you, Joy and I are just friends.'

And that 'friend' knew, even if Danny didn't, exactly why Marcus Ballantyne had decided to join the two of them. Ridiculous, she thought, not for the first time this evening. A man like Marcus Ballantyne, who could have his pick of beautiful women, couldn't possibly be seriously interested in her. Well, of course, he wasn't *seriously* interested. It was the fact that he found her attractive at all that was so unnerving. And he so obviously did. He certainly wasn't remaining with them because he enjoyed Danny's company; the slight contempt he had for the younger man was more than apparent to Joy.

'Why don't the two of you join our party?' Marcus Ballantyne invited smoothly. 'They're going on somewhere to dance,' he encouraged huskily.

Danny looked at her. 'Joy?'

She knew what Casey would say. Have fun. Enjoy yourself. Flirt a little.

But that would be so completely out of charcter. Until six months ago she had been in a steady relationship for almost four years with Gerald, a man in his late forties who took life very seriously, his career in particular. And their parting had not been an amicable one.

Even more reason to relax and enjoy herself now, Casey would have told her. *Had* told her before she came away. 'Forget your life back here for a week, Joy,' he had instructed firmly. 'Be someone else for a while, do things you wouldn't normally do. That shouldn't be too difficult,' he had added disgustedly, because she never did anything except go to work, go home to spend the evening reading, and then get up the next morning and go to work again. She hadn't even taken a day off in the last six months. She had worked six days a week, concentrating on her household chores on Sundays.

Casey had made her life sound so boring, so— so flat and mundane. And when she had sat and thought about it she had realised that it was, that she was a twenty-seven-year-old woman who was allowing life just to pass her by, who was becoming staid and old-maidish. That was the reason she had finally allowed herself to be pressured into coming away for this week...

But surely this was going to the other extreme, going off to God knew where for the rest of the evening, with a group of actors and actresses who had nothing in common with her normal everyday life? Absolutely nothing in common with that boring, flat, mundane life...

'Yes, I would like that.' She felt a surge of exhilaration, and her cheeks flushed as she voiced her impulsive decision out loud. 'I would like that very much,' she repeated firmly, that exhilaration turning to a feeling of fluttering excitement in the pit of her stomach as she saw the look of satisfaction on Marcus Ballantyne's face at her agreement to his suggestion that they go dancing.

CHAPTER TWO

'YOUR friend seems happy enough,' Marcus drawled beside her.

Joy glanced over uninterestedly to where Danny was now dancing enthusiastically with the pouting blonde.

She still wasn't quite sure what she was doing here herself, in a nightclub she had only ever read about in the newspapers before this evening, but Marcus Ballantyne was right: Danny was certainly enjoying himself with the young actress.

They had all piled into taxis when they had left the restaurant earlier, and somehow Joy had found herself squashed between the door of the taxi and Marcus Ballantyne. And he hadn't left her side since their arrival at the club, the slightly proprietorial air he had adopted towards her warning off any of the other men in the group. Including Danny, who, because of the older man's apparent interest in her, had suddenly started looking at her with new eyes himself. But after making such a point of saying they were simply old friends, he hadn't been able to make too much of a claim on her himself, finally going off to chat and flirt with the lovely blonde who had been so peeved with Marcus Ballantyne earlier. Joy was sure that initially the two of them had only got together because they were so piqued with her and Marcus, but they now seemed to be genuinely enjoying each other's company.

'Yes,' she acknowledged huskily, taking a sip of her wine, unable to look at Marcus.

God, she felt uncomfortable in his company. She didn't even know what to talk to him about!

'Relax, Joy.' As he spoke Marcus moved one lean hand to cover hers as it rested on her thigh, causing Joy to look up at him with startled green eyes. 'I'm quite harmless, you know.' He gave her that teasing grin that was so famous from television and film screens.

Anyone less harmless than this man she had yet to meet! He gave the impression of a leashed tiger, bound only by a thin veneer of civilisation. And it was questionable whether that veneer always remained in place. Somehow Joy doubted it...

Marcus leaned forward slightly, bringing his face dangerously close to hers, his fingers becoming entwined with hers now—long, lean fingers that made her hand look tiny in comparison. But everything about this man was big—in fact, he was larger than life. Joy felt lost.

'I don't bite—at least, not on a first date,' he told her huskily, dark blue eyes alight with humour.

Completely lost! She shouldn't have listened to Casey's voice inside her head earlier. She wasn't having fun and enjoying herself, was too nervous in this man's company to do that. Gerald had been old beyond his years, very serious, and so her experience with men was limited—very limited when it came to men like Marcus Ballantyne. She certainly couldn't forget who she was for this one evening, and flirt with this man. She was totally out of her depth.

She swallowed hard. 'We aren't on a date,' she dismissed, as lightly as she could, hoping she sounded more self-assured than she felt.

'That can easily be remedied.' He shrugged broad shoulders. 'Have dinner with me tomorrow evening.' His blue gaze easily held hers. 'I promise not to bite then, either.'

Have dinner with this man? Just the two of them out for an evening together? He had to be joking!

'Unless Danny was exaggerating things slightly when he told me earlier that your friendship with him was a thing of the past?' Marcus peristed at her lack of reply. 'After all, it is Valentine's night—perhaps he was trying to revive things between the two of you?'

Danny hadn't been exaggerating about there being nothing intimate between them; he had been completely fabricating the whole thing. But without revealing her own part in the competition prize, she couldn't exactly tell Marcus that. And the more time she spent in Marcus Ballantyne's company, the less she wanted him to know about that.

'There is absolutely nothing like that between Danny and myself,' she said with complete certainty, knowing there never would be. She still thought he was the biggest bore she had ever met in her life, and if she ever had to spend another evening in his company she *would* fall asleep! 'Danny was alone this evening, and I happened to be in town, so dinner seemed like a good idea,' she dismissed easily.

'Good,' Marcus accepted with satisfaction. 'In that case, think about dinner tomorrow. And in the meantime,' he added, before she could make a reply, 'would you like to dance?'

Joy very much doubted that this man very often had to leave a woman to think about going out with him! It was... Dance? He wanted her to get up and dance with him? To this? The loud rock music had stopped several minutes ago to be replaced by slow love-songs—in fact Danny and the young blonde had been entwined in each other's arms for some time. And now Marcus had suggested that the two of them——!

He gave a throaty chuckle at her side. 'I don't think I've ever met anyone quite like you before, Joy,' he told her with a smile, as she turned to look at him enquiringly. 'Believe me, you're very refreshing!' he assured her at her doubtful look.

Gauche and unsophisticated was what he really meant, Joy was sure. And who could blame him for thinking that? She was behaving like some inexperienced teenager rather than the mature woman she was supposed to be. The man was suggesting they dance together, not asking her to go to bed with him!

'I would love to dance.' She stood up determinedly once she had made the announcement, her forced confidence shaken a little as she realised that Marcus Ballantyne's fingers were still entwined with hers, his hand tightening its grasp slightly as he stood up beside her, moving forward to make a path for them to the crowded dance-floor.

Joy had no choice but to go along with him; the clasp of his hand was deceptively light, but she had no doubt that if she seemed in any danger of leaving his side, for whatever reason, his fingers would tighten quite painfully.

Her heart was racing; a pulse seemed to be hammering in her throat as Marcus took her in his arms.

He was so much taller and bigger than she was, she realised, as he gathered her close against him, the top of her head resting under his chin, strong arms about her waist as he moulded her body against his.

Joy could barely breathe—and it had little to do with the fact that her face was buried against the hardness of his chest. It had everything to do with the fact that she was completely aware of this man, from the hard leanness of his body to the tantalising smell of the aftershave he wore.

He moved rhythmically to the beat of the music, his body seductive against hers, the crush of the dance-space making it impossible for them to move off the spot. When he had pulled her into his arms Joy hadn't known what to do with her hands, but as Marcus put his arms possessively about her narrow waist she had perforce to place her hands on his broad shoulders. And she had never felt so uncomfortable in her life, her efforts to hold herself apart from Marcus quickly dealt with by him as he moulded her into the hard contours of his body with the firmness of his hands against her lower back. In fact, those hands were a little too familiar against the curve of the base of her spine!

'I said relax, Joy.' He lowered his head to murmur close to her ear, his breath warm and caressing against her skin. 'We're only dancing.'

It might only be dancing to him, but it felt more like making love to music to her! Maybe he was

used to this sort of intimacy, but she c
wasn't; there didn't seem to be a part of their b
that wasn't touching; even their legs were brush
together as they could only move from side to side
to the music. So much for behaving like the mature
woman she was supposed to be; her legs felt as if
they were going to buckle beneath her if this bat-
tering to her senses continued.

'Have fun. Enjoy yourself. Flirt a little!' This
was going from one extreme to the other. From
merely existing for the last six months—going to
work, then home, then back to work again—she
had suddenly been thrust into a situation, with this
wildly attractive man, that she just didn't know how
to deal with. She wasn't just out of her depth, she
was sinking! It reminded her of a poem she had
loved to read when she was younger, she thought
slightly hysterically, the poem a cry for help from
someone everyone thought was in control but who
was actually anything but. Her own self-assured
control had completely deserted her.

'Would you like to sit down again?' Marcus offered huskily. 'I've been wanting to hold you in my
arms like this ever since I glanced across the restaurant earlier and saw you sitting there like a
shimmering green flame among the dross,' he continued softly. 'But we can sit down if that's what
you would prefer to... God, Joy, what's a woman
like you doing with a man like Danny Eames?' He
suddenly sounded angry.

Joy gasped at this attack. 'I——'

'The man is at best an idiot,' Marcus rasped dis-
paragingly. 'At worst——'

'I don't really think it's any of your business what I'm doing with Danny,' Joy cut in, having recovered slightly from the unexpected attack. 'And what do you mean,' she added defensively, 'a woman like me?'

'You're everything that Danny isn't.' Marcus shook his head. 'You have style—something he will never have. Why are you wasting your time on a man like him?'

Joy looked up at him angrily. 'When there's someone like you around, you mean?' she scorned.

'We weren't talking about me——'

'Weren't we?' she interrupted again.

'Maybe we were,' he accepted slowly. 'Joy, you're worth a thousand of Danny Eames, don't you realise that?' he said almost angrily.

'You don't even know me,' she dismissed with derision.

'But I would like to,' he told her huskily. 'Very much so. You're beautiful, Joy. So beautiful. You... I'm going to kiss you!' he warned gruffly, seconds before his head lowered and his lips claimed hers.

Joy's hands tightened instinctively on his shoulders. The two of them had given up any impression of dancing now, and Joy was aware of nothing but the gentle exploration of Marcus's mouth against hers.

And the caress of those lips was so very, very gentle, softly exploring, the tip of his tongue lightly probing, his arms tightening about her waist now, the sound of Joy's heart thundering in her ears.

'Er—sorry to interrupt you two,' a tentative voice intruded. 'But we're moving on, and wondering if you're coming with us?'

She turned dazedly to look at Danny as Marcus reluctantly broke their kiss to raise his head and acknowledge the other man's presence with a glowering glare. What was she doing? Having fun? Enjoying herself? Flirting a little? A little! If Danny hadn't interrupted them when he had, God knew what would have happened, right here on the dance-floor!

'No,' Marcus answered the other man harshly, his arm tight about Joy's waist as he anchored her to his side. 'I'm taking Joy home,' he announced arrogantly.

'She's staying at a hotel,' Danny answered him a little dazedly, looking questioningly at Joy with raised brows.

As well he might. She had started this evening with one man, and was now apparently leaving with another one. Apparently, because she had no intention of letting Marcus take her back to her hotel. There were limits to having fun, enjoying herself, flirting a little, and she knew that she had more than reached them with Marcus. The man was dangerous—to her peace of mind, her sensibilities, to her control over a situation that was fast spiralling out of control. She hadn't even been aware of where she was a moment ago, had been completely under Marcus's sensuous spell.

'Thank you for the offer, Marcus.' She moved determinedly out of the curve of his restraining arm as she spoke. 'But Danny will take me back to my hotel.' She looked challengingly at the younger man, knowing his instinct was to bow to the superior arrogance of Marcus Ballantyne. But the challenge of her gaze obviously conveyed the message it was meant to, and Danny began to shift uncomfortably at the thought of opposing the older man. Danny owed her one, and they both knew it. 'My mother always told me it's bad manners to leave at the end of the evening with anyone other than the person you arrived with.' She had no idea whether or not her mother had ever made such a statement, but it was reasonable that she might have done.

'We arrived here as a group,' Marcus drawled mockingly, his lazily relaxed stance belied by the hard glitter in dark blue eyes; he wasn't happy at the thought of being thwarted in this way.

Well, Joy wasn't happy either at the thought of his taking her back to her hotel; she seemed to have absolutely no will-power when it came to resisting this man. And a brief fling with an actor, even one as attractive as Marcus Ballantyne, was not on the agenda for this week. And she had a feeling that if he came back to her hotel with her, after the intensity of the kisses they had already shared, taking her to bed was exactly what he would expect.

She could already hear Casey's incredulity at her not allowing that to happen, Lisa's disbelief in Joy's reluctance to become involved, however fleetingly, with a man like Marcus Ballantyne. Well, she wasn't even going to tell them about it!

'Danny and I still have a lot of gossip to catch up on.' Joy put her arm pointedly in the crook of Danny's. 'Don't we, Danny?' She looked up to give him a glowing smile, a warning light in her eyes as she did so.

'Oh, we do,' he readily agreed, nodding his head with enthusiasm, obviously warned. 'Sorry, Marcus.' He gave the other man a slightly apprehensive look, obviously fearing retribution. Joy was in no doubt that Marcus could be cutting if he chose to be.

'I have a feeling Dee won't be too happy if you disappear with Joy.' Marcus looked pointedly at the young blonde actress, who was no longer just poutingly upset at the thought of losing the second man of the evening to Joy, but obviously blazingly angry.

If Dee was lucky she would have Marcus back in her company but, whatever happened, Joy was leaving with Danny and not Marcus. 'It was nice to meet you.' Joy put her hand out to Marcus in a formal parting. 'But Danny and I really do have to go now.'

'Well, if you and Danny have to go now, I suppose you have to go,' he accepted in a hard voice, totally ignoring her outstretched hand to bend his head and lightly brush his lips against hers. 'I'll be in touch,' he told her, so softly that only Joy could hear him.

As only she had been meant to hear him! What did he mean, he would be in touch? In what way would he be in touch? He couldn't——

'Let's go,' Danny told her firmly, giving Dee a regretful smile before guiding Joy out of the nightclub.

Joy didn't even start to breathe again until they were outside, and then she drew in a ragged, much-needed gasp of air to her starved lungs. God, what a disaster, what an absolute, absolute disaster! She wished she had never come away for this week, wished she had stayed in the safety of her own little world. It was a sure fact that she didn't belong in this one!

'You haven't heard the last of him, you know.' Danny spoke softly as they travelled by taxi to her hotel.

She hadn't wanted him to put into words what she thought she already knew. 'Don't be ridiculous,' she snapped defensively, not even attempting to pretend she didn't know who he was talking about—that would have been absurd.

'I know him of old, Joy.' Danny shook his head in the half-light of the taxi. 'The only reason he wasn't more insistent just now was so that there wasn't a scene. But, above everything else, Marcus can be determined when he wants something.'

Had he been determined when he had kissed her in the middle of that crowded nightclub? Joy didn't know whether it was determination or arrogance, but she did know that Gerald would never have behaved in such an exhibitionist way. Gerald ... She hated to think what he would make of all the events of this evening and, more precisely, her own part in them!

Not that it was any of Gerald's business what she did any more. It had stopped being so six months ago, when he had chosen to break off their relationship and announce that he was going out with a woman of his own age. Joy had been stunned by his decision; after almost four years together she had believed Gerald would ask her to marry him in the near future.

But instead Gerald had begun to date a widow of forty-five, a woman with grown-up children, leaving Joy to wonder why things had gone wrong between them. But that hadn't been the worst part. Gerald was actually in charge of the library where she worked, and so Joy was also left with the humiliation of going in to work every day with the people who had known of their past relationship, and the reason it had ended so abruptly.

And Joy hadn't thought about that for weeks. Well—days. Yes, it had been days, she realised with some surprise, the preparations for this week away having taken over her life for some time before she actually came to London. So why was she thinking about that past disappointment now? She knew it had to be because of the sharp contrast between Gerald and Marcus Ballantyne; two men more unalike she had yet to meet...

'Marcus can be a very determined man, Joy,' Danny repeated, at her continued lack of reply to his statement.

She thought she already knew that, knew that Marcus had meant it when he said he would be in touch. But he had to find her first. And there was only one way he could do that... 'I want you to promise me you won't tell him which hotel I'm staying at, Danny.' She looked at him determinedly, the light of battle in sparkling green eyes.

All Danny's bravado had left him since the advent of Marcus Ballantyne into their evening, and he had the look of a hunted man on his face now. He drew in a ragged breath. 'If he asks me——'

'You aren't going to tell him,' Joy cut in firmly. 'Look, Danny, he's only playing games, and I'm not into game-playing,' she added almost angrily. She wasn't about to provide a fleeting amusement for anyone, not after what she had already been through with one man in her life.

Danny gave her a speculatively sideways glance. 'You looked as if you were enjoying yourself a few minutes ago.'

When Marcus had been kissing her. There was no denying she had been completely under his spell then, hadn't cared herself where they were or who could see them. Which was another reason she didn't want to see him again; she had to return to her normal life when this week was over, and she didn't want that to be any more difficult than it already promised to be.

'So did you,' she snapped back, relieved to see they were back at her hotel. 'Don't bother to come in, Danny; you may as well let the taxi take you on to wherever you want to go.' Probably back to the nightclub, to the beautiful Dee. Where, hopefully, Marcus wouldn't still be and see the other man's return. On second thoughts, bearing in mind her warning to Danny, which she knew he had perfectly understood, maybe Danny wouldn't go back to the nightclub...

As she expected, Danny made no move to get out of the taxi to open the door for her, a disgruntled look on his face. 'I'll see you at four o'clock tomorrow afternoon for the photographs,' he muttered sulkily.

Joy came to an abrupt halt in climbing out of the taxi. 'What photographs?' She looked at him sharply.

He shrugged, still glowering. 'It's part of the competition prize, Joy,' he explained bad-temperedly, obviously wishing he had stayed well away from the whole venture. 'Publicity for the magazine. Photographs of me with the competition winner,' he continued as she still looked at him blankly.

Casey had forgotten to mention any photographs! Well, over her dead body was she posing for photographs with this man so that all the magazine readers could drool over them curiously; every one of those women was welcome to Danny Eames as far as she was concerned.

'See you, Danny,' she told him non-committally, having no intention of being anywhere near the hotel tomorrow afternoon. Photographs, indeed! God, how humiliating.

'We have two messages for you, Miss Simms,' the receptionist of the hotel told her brightly when she collected her key.

Her heart leapt; surely Marcus hadn't found her already? No, of course he hadn't, she told herself self-derisively. There was no way he could find out which hotel she was staying at. And she was sure she could trust Danny not to tell the other man; after all, neither of them wanted Marcus to know of the competition.

'A message from a photographer about tomorrow afternoon,' the receptionist told her lightly, only raising her eyebrows slightly as Joy took the piece of paper with that message on and screwed it up into a hall. 'And the other is that a Mr Simms rang at about one-fifteen,' she smiled. 'He said he would ring again.'

'When?' Joy asked abruptly, wanting a word with Casey herself.

'He didn't specify a time,' the young receptionist told her apologetically.

Joy just bet he hadn't. Damn Casey. And she didn't need two guesses as to why he had telephoned at all; he wanted to know how she had got on with her date with Danny Eames. And as she hadn't even been back in the hotel an hour ago, when he had rung, his imagination was probably working overtime. Damn Casey! Damn Danny Eames! And, most of all, damn Marcus Ballantyne!

Because for a brief time tonight her control had slipped completely—and he had been the cause of it...

The insistent knocking finally broke through the deep realms of her sleep-muddled brain, Joy coming awake with a resistant groan. Who could be calling on her at this time of the morning...? Oh, God— a glance at the illuminated bedside clock had shown her that it was only just still morning, the clock reading eleven-fifty. Of course, it had taken her hours to fall asleep after her eventful evening, and it had already been late when she had got in, but——

The loud knocking sounded again on the door of her suite. Perhaps there was a fire? Perhaps... It was no good sitting here wondering, she had to put on her dressing-gown and go and see who it was. Only it wasn't *her* dressing-gown at all, she realised with a groan as she pulled on the grey silk robe that Lisa had lent her, along with everything else she was to wear this week. Oh, well, she was sure the staff in this hotel were used to seeing people dressed—or undressed—in all sorts of clothes.

She stumbled out of the bedroom into the lounge, noticing as she did so that the dress she had worn the night before was draped across one of the armchairs. She had undressed on her way to the bedroom when she got in last night, had just wanted to fall into bed when she got there. And then she had lain awake for hours...

Danny Eames stood outside her door, the disgruntled look on his face from the night before still there. What did he want now? It was far too early for——

'I knew you weren't going to be ready,' he said impatiently, shouldering his way into the room. 'You aren't even dressed!' he added disgustedly.

Joy frowned at him, completely unconcerned by the fact that she wasn't dressed; he shouldn't even be here, let alone criticising her appearance. 'What do you want, Danny?' she asked wearily.

'We're all waiting for you downstairs,' he told her irritably. 'We have been for the last fifteen minutes.' He glanced at his watch. 'Twenty, now!'

She shook her head. 'You've lost me, Danny.' She sighed her own impatience; she was hardly in a mood to deal with riddles. 'Who is waiting for me? And why?' Not something else to do with this competiton prize that she had no idea about?

'Don't tell me you didn't get the message about the photographic session being brought forward to this morning, because Reception said they gave it to you when you got in last night!' He scowled. 'Some of us have had to change filming schedules to get here on time, and you couldn't even be bothered to get out of bed!'

She ignored the last accusation, concentrating on what he had said about the photographic session, remembering the message from the magazine that had been waiting for her last night—a message she had screwed up to throw in the bin when she got into her suite. She had assumed it was just a reminder for her to be there, not an adjustment of the time.

'I . . . forgot to read the message,' she admitted with a self-conscious grimace.

'Forgot!' Blue eyes blazed Danny's displeasure. 'Oh, never mind,' he dismissed with an impatient shake of his head. 'Just get dressed now and——' He broke off as there was another knock on the door. 'I told them I would come and find you.' He glared in the direction of the suite door. 'Just in case you . . . weren't alone,' he added with a shrug, seeming to take in her completely dishevelled appearance for the first time. 'You are alone, aren't you?' He gave a questioning look in the direction of the bedroom.

Joy had been having trouble following his conversation—the unaccustomed wine the night before, followed by her inability to get to sleep, and then falling into a deep sleep and being woken so suddenly, were not conducive to clear thinking. But the meaning of his last comment was unmistakable.

'Of course I'm alone,' she snapped.

Danny gave a mocking nod of his head. 'I wasn't sure whether Marcus might have paid you a late-night call.'

She knew exactly what he had thought, had seen the way he had taken in her appearance, noted her dress from the night before thrown over the arm of the chair—and she didn't in the least like the assumption he had made.

'I should get that if I were you.' Danny nodded in the direction of the door as the knock sounded yet again, throwing himself down into an armchair to watch her with some amusement. 'You have some explaining to do,' he added with satisfaction.

She had intended explaining nothing, hadn't intended even to be here. She cursed herself for not reading that message from the magazine the night before; if she had, she would have made sure she was far away from the hotel this morning.

Her politely enquiring smile as she opened the door was frozen on her lips as she saw who her second visitor of the morning was. Marcus Ballantyne.

And as he looked past her into the room, to where Danny sat sprawled in an armchair, his gaze slowly returning to take in her own dishevelled appearance, it was obvious by the sudden hardening of that cobalt-blue gaze that he no longer believed either of their claims of an old friendship between them, but that he thought it was still very new!

CHAPTER THREE

'SO, DANNY,' Marcus drawled coldly, brushing past Joy as he strode uninvited into her hotel suite. The arm brushing against her caused Joy to take a step back, an action he acknowledged by the raising of one dark brow before he turned his attention back to the younger man. '*This* is the reason you're too sick to be at work today!' he taunted with hard scepticism.

Joy looked at Danny too, and noted the way his face suffused with colour at the sight of Marcus, the way he sat up guiltily. And no wonder! So much for the noble claim of changing work schedules to be here this morning; Danny had simply called in sick. And from the look on his face, if he hadn't felt sick before he certainly did now.

Danny swallowed hard, his face pale now. 'Joy and I...still had some catching up to do,' he blurted out awkwardly.

Joy stared at him open-mouthed as he said exactly the thing to make the situation seem worse—and definitely different from what it actually was. Danny wasn't just a bore, he was stupid too.

'So I see,' Marcus rasped harshly, his expression glacial now. 'And did it occur to you, Danny——' the words were bitten out like darts flying between the two men, each one making its target '—that you have inconvenienced a lot of other people today

40

because of your supposed sickness? Including myself,' he added softly. Too softly.

Danny gave a nervously dismissive smile. 'You're exaggerating, Marcus——'

'Am I?' the other man returned evenly, the calmness of his exterior belied by the blazing anger in his eyes. 'I don't think so, Danny,' he bit out tautly. 'As you must have known, we had to re-schedule all this morning's scenes. And all because you, apparently, couldn't be bothered to get out of bed with your old friend Joy!'

She gasped her indignation at the accusation. How dared he? Who did he think he...? She bit her bottom lip in agitation as Marcus bent down to pick up the shimmering green dress she had been wearing the night before, looking at it scathingly before holding it out to her. Joy took the dress un-thinkingly, clasping it to her, well aware herself now of exactly how damning this situation looked.

But she didn't owe anyone an explanation—even if what Marcus was thinking about Danny and herself had been true. She could understand Marcus being annoyed with Danny for not being at work this morning, but on a personal basis it was none of his business whether Danny had spent the night here with her or not. And that was the only side of this that concerned her; Danny would have to get himself out of the other scrape he had got himself into.

'I'm going to get dressed,' she abruptly told no one in particular, looking at neither man as she walked towards the bedroom, hoping—she knew futilely—that both men would have left by the time she returned.

'That might be a good idea,' Marcus said coldly behind her.

Her back stiffened at the insult she could hear in his voice, and she quickly made good her escape into the bedroom. And it did feel like an escape; the air in the other room had been electric with angry disapproval. As had Marcus himself. She had no idea why he was here, how he had found her hotel, but she knew all three of them wished he hadn't.

God, what a disaster! It was stupid of Danny to have told such a lie. Even more stupid of him to be caught out in it in such a way. And even more stupid than anything else to involve her in the lie in the way he had! Oh, she was involved, as far as being the winner of the competition went, but the impression he had given Marcus had been of something completely different between them.

And after all that she had said to Marcus the night before about Danny and her just being old friends. Maybe sometimes old friends did go to bed together, but she and Danny weren't old anything; after the mess he had just made of things, she knew they never would be either. How on earth either of them was going to be able to talk themselves out of this one, she just didn't know.

She felt decidedly more comfortable once she had dressed in close-fitting denims with a black jumper neatly tucked in at her narrow waist, brushed her hair loosely about her shoulders, and applied a light make-up to add some colour to her pale cheeks. She had a feeling she was going to need all the confidence she could muster to get through the next few minutes. Surely that was all it would take for

Marcus to tell the two of them exactly what he thought of them—if he hadn't already—and be on his way.

She took a deep breath before reaching to turn the door-handle to go back into the lounge. Both men hadn't gone—but Danny had, damn him!

Marcus stood alone in the room. He had made no move to take off the thick short coat that he wore over a dark blue shirt and fitted denims, despite the heat of the hotel suite. Good, perhaps that meant he wasn't staying long either. Just long enough to tell her what he thought of her part in Danny's absence this morning, probably!

He looked at her from beneath dark scowling brows, his eyes darkly glacial, his mouth a thin, grim line. Joy shifted uncomfortably under that probing gaze.

'How did you find my hotel?' she asked, once she could stand the lengthy silence no longer.

He remained unmoving. 'That was the easy part,' he bit out.

In other words, that was for him to know and for her only to guess. And the only explanation she could think of was that he had tried all the main hotels until he had found the one she was staying at. It was just like him not to have announced his imminent arrival too; if he had, the previous scene with Danny would never have happened.

She interlaced her hands in front of her thighs, mainly as a way of hiding the fact that they were shaking slightly, but also because she just didn't know what to do with them; she felt so uncomfortable facing Marcus across the room like this. He wasn't at all the man she had spent some of the previous evening with—the danger that emanated from him now was certainly not of the sensual kind.

'Er—where's Danny?' she said, really more for something to say than from any real interest in where the other man had gone. But she could see by the increased tightness of Marcus's jaw that it had been the wrong thing to say.

'He had to leave. Obviously,' Marcus added harshly.

Joy didn't see that there was anything obvious about it; Danny should have stayed here and helped her out of this situation. But she should have known that he wouldn't; he was terrified of the older man.

'Oh.' She nodded lightly, turning away.

'But I have no doubt he'll be back,' Marcus added contemptuously.

Neither did Joy, if only to see what conversation had taken place between herself and Marcus once he had left—and just how he had fitted into it. Well, he should have stayed if he wanted to know that, not left her at this man's mercy.

'Why the lies, Joy?' Marcus rasped harshly, causing Joy to look up at him in fresh alarm. 'Are you married? Is that it? A married woman in London, away from hubby, out for a little fun with her actor-friend?'

He spoke so contemptuously, looked at her so disgustedly...! And by what right? she wanted to know, if all she had ever read about him was true.

'Don't judge everyone by your own standards!' she snapped, green eyes sparkling with anger as she glared at him.

He became very still, eyes narrowed to steely slits. 'Meaning?' he prompted, in that dangerously soft voice she was quickly learning to be wary of.

But not at this moment. Who did he think he was, coming here throwing out accusations? He had kissed her himself last night, on a very brief acquaintance, so who was he to sit in judgement of what he thought she and Danny had done last night?

'Meaning your affairs, with married as well as unmarried women, are legendary!' she told him heatedly. She might not be interested in the gossip from his world, but it had become impossible over the years not to see his photograph in newspapers and magazines, each time with a different woman. And he had the nerve to sit in judgement of her and Danny!

This was ridiculous; she was allowing herself to be indignant about a supposed affair that she knew didn't even exist. And the quicker she told him that, the sooner he would leave.

But before she could say anything he had crossed the room in two long strides, his hands reaching out to grasp her painfully by the tops of her arms. Joy was so stunned by the suddenness of his action that she could only stare up at him in open-mouthed surprise.

'In that case,' he ground out harshly, 'it won't matter if I add one more to my list, will it?'

Her? He——

There was no time for further thought as his mouth came down on hers with crushing intensity, Marcus showing her none of the gentleness of the night before as his mouth claimed hers bruisingly, his arms about her waist moulding the curves of her body roughly against his.

And if he had continued to kiss her in that contemptuous way, she would have been able to pull away from him and end it right then. But, filled with sudden anger as the kiss had begun, it just as suddenly gentled to sensuous intensity, and one of Marcus's hands moved to cup her chin as he held her mouth captive beneath his and sipped from her lips, touching softly now, the tip of his tongue a moist caress to the warmth of her mouth.

Joy knew the same mindless pleasure as she had felt last night, couldn't think, had no desire for anything but for Marcus to go on kissing her. Her arms moved up about his neck as she held him to her, her body bending into his with boneless need.

'God, Joy! You're beautiful. Beautiful!' he murmured heatedly against her throat, his lips moist and hot, making her quiver with arousal. 'And I want you,' he added raggedly, raising his head to look down at her with intensely dark blue eyes, a flush on his hard cheeks.

Joy knew he wanted her, wasn't so inexperienced that she couldn't feel the pulsing desire in his body and recognise it for what it was. And it was a desire that was echoed in her own body. The anger between them had quickly turned to throbbing need, and Joy's hands clung to his shoulders as much to stop herself falling as to feel the broad strength of him.

Marcus looked into her face searchingly. 'You want me too,' he finally groaned. 'Joy!' His mouth claimed hers once again.

Their kisses became more intense, more desperate, desire spiralling out of control now as one of Marcus's hands moved to cup her breast, Joy gasping in pleasure as his thumb moved rhythmically against the already hardened nipple, a heat she had never known before coursing through her body.

She offered no resistance whatsoever when Marcus swept her up in his arms and carried her over to the sofa, sitting down with her still in his arms as he laid her back against the cushions. Joy's eyes were closed as she revelled in the sensuous pleasure heating her body, but her eyes opened wide as she felt Marcus's lips against the nakedness of her pulsing breast, lips that slowly explored until her eyes closed again in an ecstasy she had never known before. Her nipple was between his lips now, his tongue moving wetly over that hardened tip as he roused her to a frenzy of passion totally unknown to her. And so irresistible . . . !

His hands moved restlesly against her thighs, moulding her to him as he moved his body on top of hers, nestling between her legs, denim against denim, as their bodies fitted perfectly together. Joy looked down at Marcus now, his hair dark against her milky-white skin, his eyes dark with sensuous passion, and he raised his head only high enough to be able to look at her, her nipple still his captive, their gazes clashing and holding as each saw the burning desire in blue and green depths.

It was the most erotic experience to look at Marcus as he was kissing her breast; one of her hands moved up to cradle his head against her, never wanting the caress to end, her body so heated with desire that she felt about to explode.

Marcus saw the pleasure in her eyes and his mouth slowly left her nipple; all the time he was watching her as his tongue moved between his lips to begin a slow moist exploration of that hardened tip of her breast.

She was so hot. With needing. And wanting. Wanting Marcus. Wanting the hardness of his body to claim hers, to complete her pleasure, to take her to the heights her own body cried out for, heights she knew Marcus could show her...

'Please!' she groaned mindlessly, her hands tangled in the darkness of his hair as his lips claimed her other nipple now, while his hand continued to caress the moist tip of the one he had just pleasured. Her body was shaking with need, with a heat that had to be assuaged. With a need for Marcus, all of him...

'Tell me, Joy——' his breath was hot against her heat-dampened skin '—tell me you want me.'

How could he doubt it? Every nerve-ending, every part of her, cried out her need for him.

'Want *me*, I mean, Joy,' he continued raggedly. 'Say "I want you, Marcus".' He cradled her face with his hands, his gaze holding her captive now as he willed her to echo his words.

She didn't understand. How could he doubt...? No, he couldn't possibly mean...!

She stared up at him with horror dawning in her eyes. He did mean exactly what she had realised; he didn't want her to be at all mistaken about the lover in her arms, wanted her to say his name, believed——

Saved by the bell! Or was she? The ringing telephone had certainly halted the anguished outburst in her throat. But who had it saved? Certainly not her, because after what Marcus had just said the passion and desire inside her had died as suddenly as they had coursed through her body, and she was now shocked at her own abandon, covered with confusion at her uninhibited response. She had acted like a wanton——

'I'll get that,' Marcus muttered roughly, turning away to pick up the telephone receiver.

Joy was glad of the few seconds' respite from his probing gaze to pull her clothing back into order, swinging her legs to put her feet back on the carpeted floor—and hopefully back onto safe ground. She smoothed back her tousled hair, colour flooding her cheeks as she remembered it had been Marcus's hands entangled in the silky mass that had caused the disorder.

'For you.' He turned to hold the receiver out to her. 'A man,' he added harshly, his mouth a thin angry line. 'Another one.'

Joy took the receiver from him, watching apprehensively as he stood up to cross the room to stare out of the window, before raising the receiver to her own ear. 'Yes?' she said reluctantly, expecting the people from the magazine to be on the other end of the line—to complain about her non-appearance this morning. After all, there weren't too many people who knew she was here at all.

'Joy!' Casey greeted enthusiastically. 'Considering you weren't even back last night when I called, I have no need to ask what sort of evening—and night—you had!'

Her cousin! He was the last person, positively the last person, she wanted to talk to just now.

'Can I call you back?' she said woodenly, all the time keeping an eye on Marcus as he stood so rigidly with his back towards her, although no doubt he could hear all her side of this telephone conversation, at least.

'Oh, come on, Joy,' Casey whined complainingly. 'How much longer to do you intend to keep me in suspense?'

'I intended returning your call later,' she told him distantly.

'But I'm here now,' he said impatiently. 'And I can't wait any longer to hear just how you got on with your date last night.'

'You'll have to,' she told him sharply, wishing he would just get off the telephone. Then she could ask Marcus to leave.

'I've taken time out of my lunch-hour to make this call,' Casey said impatiently. 'You could at least give me a clue—although maybe I have one,' he suddenly realised. 'Who's the man that answered the phone, Joy? I assumed it was someone from the hotel, but... Who is it, Joy?' he said excitedly. 'Surely not Danny Eames?'

'Certainly not!' She glanced across at Marcus after her instinctive denial—only to find he was watching her with narrowed blue eyes. Her hand tightened about the receiver. 'Look, I've said I'll call you back later,' she told Casey firmly. 'And that's exactly what I'll do.' She put the reciever firmly back in its cradle before Casey could so much as utter a protest. If he telephoned straight back she would——

'Your husband?'

She looked across at Marcus with a frown. And then she remembered the accusations he had made to her before—before—— Well, before. He really believed she was a married woman, in London having fun with a string of lovers!

She stood up abruptly. 'I don't think that is any of your business,' she told him coldly, all memory of desire for this man gone now as she looked at him so dismissively. The memories would come back later, when she was alone... 'I think you should leave now,' she added distantly.

'I intend to,' he bit out contemptuously. 'But you're good, Joy, I give you that.' He shook his head with self-disgust.

'Good?' she echoed forwningly.

He nodded. 'I really believed I had met someone different last night. You seemed so fresh and un-affected, not at all like the people I usually meet. Perhaps you should be the actress!'

'And perhaps you should meet a different crowd of people!' she told him heatedly, hurt, in spite of herself, that he could actually believe her naïveté last night had all been an act.

His mouth twisted. 'I think not. At least I know them for what they are.'

The look he gave her told her he considered that he also knew her for what she was now. 'I think you should leave now, Marcus,' she bit out tautly. He had to leave before she began to cry! Reaction to what had taken place between them a few minutes ago was starting to set in, and she now felt totally humiliated at her own weakness in being attracted to this man, in allowing that attraction to take over in the way it had.

She had never behaved in such a wanton way in her life before; her relationship with Gerald had certainly never been on that level. Maybe if it had... But no, it was too late for thoughts like that. And certainly not now. Now she just had to make Marcus leave!

'I intend to.' He nodded abruptly. 'After all, you have so many telephone calls to make—don't you?' he added contemptuously.

To the string of lovers he seemed to think she had in London. And he also thought she had decided to add him to their number. Maybe her behaviour a few minutes ago had been a little... There was no maybe about it, she inwardly admonished herself; she *had* behaved in a way that could be mistaken for none other than what it was. But, even so, Marcus had no right to jump to the assumptions about her marital status that he had. Not even when it was so obvious that she and Danny were hiding something...? No! He still didn't have that right as far as she was concerned.

'Just go,' she said wearily.

He picked up the jacket he must have discarded sometime during their lovemaking, shrugging his broad shoulders into it. 'You're playing a dangerous game, Joy,' he warned softly. 'Especially with someone like Danny. He isn't the most discreet of people,' he explained his warning about the younger man.

'And I suppose you are?' she scorned, eyes sparkling.

'Privately, yes. Publicly——' he shrugged '—I don't have the same freedom.'

She knew that only too well; she had noticed the way people looked at him in recognition last night when they were all at the nightclub together.

'And another thing, Joy.' Marcus paused as he reached the door. 'Don't believe everything you read in the newspapers,' he added softly when she looked at him enquiringly. 'I was a happily married man until my wife died five years ago,' he continued grimly. 'And, since that time, any woman in the company of whom I spend more than five minutes is reputed to be my latest mistress. If there had been any reporters at the club last night, there would have been a photograph in the newspapers this morning of the two of us together. And we both know we aren't having an affair.'

Only because of the interruption of a telephone call, Joy acknowledged miserably. But she had forgotten about his marriage. She remembered now that he had been married to the actress Rebecca Booker, who had died while making an adventure film whan a stunt had gone sadly wrong. That couldn't have been an easy time for him, she accepted.

Although that still didn't give him the right to come here making assumptions and accusations about her!

'Or ever likely to be,' she replied firmly. She doubted they would ever meet again.

Marcus shook his head. 'Why don't you go home to your husband, Joy?' He frowned. 'Danny has nothing to offer you but a good time.'

She looked at him challengingly, her head up, her hair cascading down her back. 'I thought that was what you said I was obviously in London for!' she reminded him scathingly.

He quirked dark brows. 'And are you?'

That had been the idea of her coming here, according to Casey: a time when she could forget Gerald, and the awful futility of continuinig to work with him, a time when she could forget herself for a while and become someone else. And last night she had attempted to do just that. But after meeting Marcus, it was all turning out to be rather a nightmare, an unforeseeable nightmare...

'It hasn't been too good so far,' she acknowledged heavily, thinking of the disasters that had so far befallen her. How on earth could she, a rural librarian, have become involved with two men like Danny Eames and Marcus Ballantyne? It was totally ridiculous!

Marcus's mouth tightened, his expression grim. 'In that case, I suggest you call back the lover on the telephone just now and see if he's any improvement.' With one last contemptuous look in her direction, he wrenched open the door, closing it forcefully behind him as he left.

The room still seemed charged with his presence even after he had gone. Joy's breath left her lungs with a shuddering sigh as she sank down weakly into one of the armchairs. What a mess, an absolute mess.

And, although it might have been Casey's idea that she come to London in the first place, she really had no one else but herself to blame for what had happened just now...

CHAPTER FOUR

'SMILE, damn it!' Danny growled at her out of the corner of his mouth. 'If anyone has reason to look sick of all this, it's me.' Despite his obvious ill-humour, the teasingly boyish grin stayed on his lips as his face remained directed at the camera across the room.

Professionalism, Joy supposed it was called. But she had no reason even to attempt to look happy about this situation. She had been too dazed after Marcus's departure from her hotel suite to do more than sit in her room and try to gather her chaotic thoughts together. That had been a mistake. The representative from the magazine, obviously tiring of the wait downstairs, had taken that opportunity to come and find her. And the photographic session had been rescheduled for this evening...

Danny had looked no more happy about it than she had when he arrived half an hour ago—in fact, he looked decidedly green. But there had been no opportunity for the two of them to talk privately together, so Joy had no idea what was wrong with him. Although she had an idea it might have been another encounter with Marcus...

Not that she particularly wanted to hear about that; she was still shaken by what had happened between herself and Marcus. The two men would have to sort out their own differences, definitely without any help from her.

They had set up the photographic session in one of the luxurious lounges of the hotel, and, after looking through Joy's wardrobe, the magazine representative had chosen the backless black gown as the one she would like Joy to wear. Seen from the front it was quite a demure dress, except for its exceptionally short skirt, but her back was bare almost down to the base of her spine—making it impossible for her to wear any underwear at all except the briefest pair of black briefs. Joy had to admit that it was a beautiful dress, and her hair looked like a cascade of flame down her spine, once the hairdresser had got to work. But, nevertheless, she felt uncomfortable in such a revealing dress, and couldn't wait for the photographs to be over with so that she could go and change into something less—eyecatching.

But Danny had other ideas, grabbing hold of her arm and dragging her towards the hotel bar once all the people from the magazine had left. His grip was quite painful, digging into her bare flesh, the dress being sleeveless as well as backless, and Joy was relieved when they reached the comfort of the bar and he released her to go and get them both a drink.

'I know it wasn't much fun, Danny——' Joy eyed him as he drank down what appeared to be a double whisky in just two swallows '—but it wasn't that bad.' In fact, she had quite enjoyed the experience of being photographed, once she had accepted the fact that there was no way she could get out of it. 'Besides,' she added lightly, 'you should be used to it.'

Danny eyed her malevolently across the width of the coffee-table that separated them as they sat in armchairs in the bar area. 'I may have to get *un*used to it!' His scowl deepened.

Joy frowned too now. 'What do you——?'

'Excuse me.' He stood up abruptly. 'I need another drink.'

As he walked back to the bar, she watched him, making no attempt to drink the glass of white wine he had brought back for her last time. Danny had been bad-tempered ever since his arrival here this evening; in fact, he had been decidedly morose until he had stepped in front of the camera, at which time he had become completely professional, smiling and laughing for the photographs. But there was obviously something seriously wrong with him and, much as Joy found him a pain and a bore, if his bad temper was due to Marcus, then she probably had something to do with it, and so was partly responsible.

'What's wrong, Danny?' she prompted gently, once he had sat down with his second drink in as many minutes.

'Wrong?' he echoed sarcastically. 'What could possibly be wrong?' he dismissed scornfully. 'I'm about to be... About to be!' he repeated disgustedly. 'I have been!' He shook his head, staring down into the bottom of his whisky-glass as he swirled the contents around uninterestedly.

Joy frowned. 'Have been what?'

He looked up to glare at her with blazing blue eyes. 'Axed from *Pilgrim's Game*,' he ground out harshly, taking another swallow of the whisky.

She stared at him. *Pilgrim's Game* was the name of the series he and Marcus starred in, Pilgrim being the name of the leading character that Marcus played. Danny played the part of the sergeant who accompanied him on his cases. How could Danny have been axed from such a part?

'Don't look so surprised.' He gave a bitter laugh. 'Marcus made it pretty clear this morning just how angry he was.'

She nodded, still dazed. 'Because you called in sick and they had to reschedule.'

Danny's mouth twisted scornfully. 'You don't think that's really what all this is about, do you?' He gave her a pitying look.

He couldn't be saying he had been sacked from the series because Marcus had found the two of them together in her hotel suite this morning? Surely not? Marcus was a powerful figure in the acting world, but surely even he didn't have the power to... It sounded too incredible.

'Grow up, Joy,' Danny derided scathingly as the incredulity slowly spread across her face. 'Marcus is the star and what he says, where *Pilgrim's Game* is concerned, goes.'

She didn't think now was the time to point out to him that last night he had been claiming the series couldn't even exist without him in it! There had to be some sort of mistake, though, she was sure; Marcus might be a lot of things—and some of them she would prefer not to think about—but she hadn't seen him as a vindictive man. But there was no disputing the fact that Danny appeared to have been dropped from the series the other man starred in...

'Have you tried talking to Marcus?' She still frowned.

'About what?' Danny dismissed bitterly. 'My agent has been told my contract ends with the end of this series. It's not negotiable.'

It did sound pretty conclusive, but surely...? Oh, she didn't for a moment believe the series couldn't run without Danny, but, even so, he was a fundamental part of the programme, and surely couldn't just be written out in this sudden way. And, like Danny, she couldn't help feeling it was too much of a coincidence that he had only been told about it this afternoon; it must have something to do with Marcus finding them in her suite together this morning. And she wasn't happy about her part in this at all.

'Where does Marcus live, Danny?' she asked him firmly.

Now it was his turn to frown. 'What on earth do you want to know that for?'

'Maybe the two of us should go and talk to him,' she said determinedly, the light of battle in sparkling green eyes.

If her being with Danny did have anything to do with this, she intended setting the record straight— as well as telling Marcus exactly what she thought of him and his power-games. Her supposed friendship with Danny was their own affair—and an affair was exactly what Marcus believed it to be!—and shouldn't have anything to do with Danny's professional life.

Danny shifted in his seat. 'I don't want to see him just now,' he muttered. 'The mood I'm in, I might just hit him,' he added disgustedly. 'And after that he would probably make sure I never worked again.'

Hearing the way his words were slightly slurred, seeing the slight flush in his cheeks, where the alcohol was taking effect, Joy thought perhaps Danny might be right about not seeing Marcus himself just now. She had no doubt which man would emerge the victor in any physical fight between Danny, even stone-cold sober, and Marcus, and with Danny more than slightly drunk there wouldn't even be a contest; Marcus would lay the other man out cold.

'Very well.' She nodded briskly. 'Then I'll go and talk to him on my own.' Even as she said the words she felt a fluttering of apprehension in the pit of her stomach; she had no desire ever to see Marcus again, and was still shaken by her uninhibited response to him this morning. But if those events of this moring did have some bearing on Danny being sacked from the series, then she had something to say about it!

Danny looked at her with brows raised. 'What happened between the two of you this morning after I left?' he asked speculatively.

There was no way she could prevent the colour that entered her cheeks. 'That has nothing to do with this——'

'Doesn't it?' Danny eyed her consideringly. 'I think perhaps it might,' he said slowly.

So did she, which was why she felt she should at least try to talk to Marcus on Danny's behalf—otherwise she wouldn't ever go near him again. Marcus was a danger to her own peace of mind, affected her in a way she had never been before, reduced her self-control to tatters.

'Just tell me where he lives, Danny,' she said wearily. 'At least then we'll know whether or not Marcus did have something to do with you being axed from the series.'

'Of course he did,' Danny insisted heatedly. 'He——'

'His address, Danny,' she cut in. 'You can stay here, if you like, while I go and talk to him.' It shouldn't take too long; a simple yes or no to her question would be sufficient.

Danny nodded. 'As it happens, I do know where Marcus lives, but only because all the cast were invited to a party there at the beginning of the first series.' He scowled.

In other words, the two men weren't usually on social terms. Not that it surprised Joy; the two men seemed to have little in common, except the fact that they were both actors. And the location of Marcus's apartment didn't come as any surprise to Joy either when Danny told it to her; it was in the most prestigious residential part of London.

Danny was still scowling after he had told her the address. 'I think I'll get myself another drink——'

'Is that a good idea?' Joy reasoned exasperatedly. She could just see the headlines in the newspaper now: 'Axed T.V. star drunk at exclusive hotel!' No, another drink for Danny wasn't a good idea. 'Go up to my suite.' She handed him the key. 'And wait for me there.' At least this way he might be lucid enough for her to talk to when she got back from seeing Marcus. Oh, God...Marcus. She didn't particularly want to go and see the other man herself—her heart was sinking at the thought of it— but what real choice did she have?

'OK,' Danny agreed—but he looked far from happy with the idea. 'Do you think you'll be long?'

He was like a churlish little boy, Joy acknowledged exasperatedly. She was doing this for him, for goodness' sake! 'As long as it takes, Danny,' she snapped, standing up. 'Just go up to my suite and wait for me there.'

She waited in the hotel long enough to see Danny lurch out of the bar and into the lift, watching the lights go on above the lift to make sure he had the right floor. He obviously did; the lift stopped at the third floor. She shook her head as she walked outside to get a taxi. Danny was so irresponsible. But at least he might have sobered up a little when she got back; she had ordered coffee to be sent up to her suite for just that purpose.

Once in the taxi she began to realise exactly what she was doing, that sinking feeling coming back into her stomach. What was she actually going to say to Marcus when she got there? They hadn't exactly parted on good terms this morning, and he was going to wonder what on earth she was doing there.

By the time the taxi arrived outside his apartment building, she still didn't quite know how she was going to start the conversation with Marcus; a lot of that would depend on Marcus's reaction to her being there at all. And, after the things he had said to her this morning, she didn't exactly think he was going to be pleased to see her again. Well, damn him. He couldn't treat Danny like this just because he was angry with her. *If* that was the reason he was being so objectionable with Danny, she reasoned to herself again; wasn't that exactly what she had come here to find out? Prejudging the situation wasn't going to help anything.

Not that Marcus was going to be surprised by her standing outside the door of his apartment, she quickly discovered, when she entered the building to find a security man sitting at a desk inside the foyer, obviously placed there for the very purpose of keeping out unwanted guests. Joy's problem was that, after this morning, she had a feeling she might fall into that category.

She should have realised that Marcus would choose to live in a place with such security; he could hardly have unwanted fans arriving on the doorstep day and night. Nevertheless, she found it a little intimidating having to give her name to the security man and then wait to see if she was to be given permission to enter.

She pretended an interest in a painting on one of the walls while the man telephoned up to Marcus's apartment to tell him of her presence—pretended, because she was actually listening to the security man's side of the conversation.

'A Miss Simms, Mr Ballantyne,' the man told him formally. 'Yes. Yes, she is. Very well, Mr Ballantyne.'

Not exactly enlightening, Joy decided. 'Very well, Mr Ballantyne'—what? Very well she was to go up to the apartment, or she wasn't?

'You can go up, Miss Simms,' the man informed her lightly.

Thank God for that. She breathed an inward sigh of relief. How humiliating to be turned away!

The security man smiled at her, seemingly unaware of her nervousness. 'Mr Ballantyne's apartment is on the top floor.' He indicated the lift across the foyer.

A penthouse apartment, no less. She should have guessed that too, she supposed. And obviously the man on the desk knew she had never been here before tonight, otherwise he wouldn't have needed to tell her which floor Marcus's apartment was on.

She still had no idea, as she travelled up in the lift, what she was going to say to Marcus when she got there, especially now that he had been warned of her arrival. Although, in truth, he couldn't be any less aware of her purpose in being there than she was of what she was actually going to say.

Stepping straight out of the lift into a reception area with a large round table with a huge vase of flowers in the centre, and four unmarked doors, one in each wall of the room, was not helpful. Which apartment was Marcus's?

'Good-evening, Joy.'

She was so startled by the unexpected sound of his voice that she almost dropped her handbag, turning sharply to the right to see him standing in the middle of a corridor she hadn't seen there, so intent had she been on those four unmarked doors.

And there didn't seem to be a door into that corridor, so what...?

'This is the penthouse apartment, Joy,' he drawled, at her obvious confusion.

All of this floor was the penthouse apartment? But the building was enormous! Which meant this apartment was likewise, she realised resignedly. She had known from the outset that Marcus inhabited a different world from her own, so why should the size of his apartment have come as such a surprise to her? It didn't, if she thought about it logically. Although it was still a huge apartment for one man...

'I live alone, Joy,' he told her, 'and have done so since my wife died.'

She wished he would stop reading her mind in that way. Was she so damned transparent? She hoped not, because the sight of him in casual black jeans and a black silk shirt, unbuttoned at the throat, was having a strange effect on her pulse-rate, and she was sure her face was flushed with the attraction towards him that she didn't seem to be able to control.

'Come through to the lounge,' he added almost wearily at her wooden silence, indicating she was to precede him down the corridor.

Joy had never seen a room like the large one she entered a few seconds later; the chairs and carpet were all cream-coloured, the other furniture all chrome and glass. But it was the outer wall of the room that held her attention, because it was completely made up of glass doors that led out on to an illuminated balcony. And even from inside the room she could see London spread out before her, seeming to reflect the starlit sky in a glittering array of lights.

'It's wonderful,' she breathed appreciatively, her gaze riveted on the almost ethereal beauty of the city.

'The estate agent brought me round to view on a night exactly like this four years ago,' he remarked drily from behind her.

Too close behind her for Joy's comfort. She didn't look round to see just how close he was, taking what she hoped was a natural-looking step forward in order to see the view better.

If Marcus had moved here four years ago, then it had been after his wife died. No doubt there were too many memories in the home the two of them had shared together. Although Joy sometimes thought that had to be a comfort to the person left behind. Obviously Marcus wasn't the type of man to need that sort of comfort.

'Let me take your jacket.' He spoke close to her again, and Joy realised he must have moved towards those glass doors with her.

She also realised that she was still wearing the black dress from the photographic session, that she had merely pulled on her black jacket over the top of it to come and see Marcus. And if she took the jacket off...

'No, I'm fine, thanks...' She had turned sharply as she spoke, and suddenly found herself dangerously close to Marcus—so close that it was impossible to look away from the dark blue depths of his eyes. 'I'm fine,' she repeated weakly.

God, this was ridiculous. This man had left her hotel at lunchtime today after throwing several more than insulting remarks at her about what he considered to be her questionable morals, and yet she could still feel attracted to him!

She drew herself up stiffly. 'I'm really fine.' She moved away from him to walk over and sit down in one of the cream leather armchairs, crossing one silken leg over the other—and then wishing she hadn't as it drew Marcus's gaze to their shapely length. 'I'm here to talk to you about Danny,' she told him bluntly.

A shutter came down over his eyes, his mouth a thin, disapproving line. 'What about him?'

Ice. Cold, unfathomable ice. This was going to be more difficult than she had imagined. And she had imagined it as being bad enough!

She drew in a ragged breath. 'I saw him to-night——'

'Your old friend?' Marcus cut in tauntingly.

Joy glared at him, green sparks seeming to flash in her eyes. 'Danny says he's been axed from *Pilgrim's Game*——'

'Does he indeed?' Marcus again interrupted her, this time softly, dangerously. 'What else did he say?'

Joy looked at him closely, wondering exactly what she had said to anger him now. And he was angry. Very much so. There was no mistaking the narrowed eyes and firm, uncompromising mouth. 'I——'

'Would you like a glass of wine while we talk about this?' he cut in yet again. 'I have a feeling we might both need it.'

Joy thought longingly of the glass of wine back in the hotel bar that she had hardly touched. If she had drunk some of it she might not be shaking quite as badly as she was now. 'A glass of wine would be...nice. Thank you,' she added abruptly.

Marcus gave a curt inclination of his head, moving over to a large cabinet that was quickly revealed as a bar, once he had opened the mirrored doors. Joy watched him for several seconds as he took a bottle of wine from the cooler and deftly removed the cork before reaching for two glasses.

As he reached upward for the glasses the silk material of his shirt stretched tautly across his back, muscles rippling there, his back broad and powerful, as were his shoulders.

Joy could remember the pleasure of the feel of that muscled back beneath her fingertips, heat instantly suffusing her body while the memory became more vivid as he bent his head over the task of pouring the wine. Her fingers had been tangled in the dark hair at his nape only hours ago. Oh, God!

'Here.' Marcus stood in front of her now, holding out one of the beautiful crystal glasses to her. And somehow Joy knew the choice of golden white wine hadn't been a random one, that Marcus had remembered she drank only white wine the evening before; he was a man who would forget little.

Which made her feel uncomfortable all over again. If she was remembering what had happened between them earlier today, then he must remember it too.

'You're looking very hot,' he remarked softly. 'Perhaps you should take your jacket off after all?'

And reveal even though her back was firmly wedged up against the chair now, that the black dress she wore was positively backless? She didn't think so. 'I'm fine as I am,' she insisted stubbornly, taking the glass of wine, careful not to come into contact with the lean fingers of his hand as she did so, gratefully swallowing some of the cool liquid.

'It's supposed to be sipped, not thrown back like a glass of beer.' Marcus watched her with wry amusement.

She put the glass down awkwardly on the table in front of her, wincing as glass met glass with a loud chinking noise. But luckily she had broken neither the top of the table nor the wine-glass. 'Sorry,' she muttered, a little irritably. Once again she was so completely out of her depth with this man, she couldn't help feeling resentful.

He nodded acknowledgement of the apology, moving to sit in the chair opposite hers across the table, cradling his wine-glass in both hands as he looked across at her over its rim. 'You were saying Danny has told you about the changes in the series...?' he prompted mildly.

Joy didn't trust his mood one little bit. There was something too calm about it, too—too... She didn't know quite what it was; she just knew she didn't trust it. The nearest thing she could think of to describe his mood was the calm before the storm, the waiting for a time bomb to go off. Not a very comfortable feeling at all.

She swallowed hard. 'He's naturally very...upset at being dropped from the series,' she said gruffly.

'Naturally.' Marcus nodded slowly, the steadiness of that dark blue gaze very unnerving on her flushed face.

'I... It's all very sudden,' Joy continued determinedly.

Marcus pursed his lips. 'You think so?'

'Well, of course it is.' She was becoming more than a little impatient with his patronising tone now. 'Danny is your co-star in the series.'

He nodded again. 'He has been, I'll grant you that.'

This wasn't going at all as she had hoped. Marcus was proving very difficult to talk to, giving away nothing himself. Not that she should really have expected anything else. But in the face of his enigmatism, Joy quite simply didn't know how to get around to making any accusations concerning his own part in Danny being axed.

'Surely it's unusual just to drop the co-star of a series like that?' she persisted, leaning forward to pick up her glass and take another sip of wine. She hadn't had any dinner yet this evening, and she rarely drank wine when she was at home, so the effects of the little she had already drunk were starting to give her some Dutch courage. Why did this particular man unnerve her so? she thought resentfully.

'A little ... drastic, I'll grant you,' Marcus acknowledged, his gaze still steady as he made no move to drink his own wine but simply looked at her over the top of the glass. It was damned annoying, she decided. And extremely unnerving. 'But it has been done before,' he added with a dismissive shrug.

Joy was sure it had, but possibly the reasons for it having been done before weren't quite the same. 'Danny believes ...' She paused, chewing on her bottom lip. 'And I happen to agree with him——'

'That must be a first,' Marcus drawled mockingly. 'I've never known anyone agree with Danny Eames before,' he explained at her questioning look.

Really, this man was impossible! She didn't like Danny any more than Marcus appeared to, but that really wasn't the point at issue here. Though she rarely watched television, even she had seen *Pilgrim's Game* several times over the couple of years it had been running, and from what she remembered, Danny played a very good part. He might be an egotistical bore to spend time with, but as an actor he obviously had some talent. Not as much as he thought he did, but, nevertheless, being axed from the series seemed a little drastic.

She drew in a determined breath. 'Danny seems to think you might have had something to do with his...demise.' She looked at him challengingly.

Marcus returned her gaze steadily, dark blue clashing with emerald-green as he seemed to look into her very soul.

This had been a mistake, Joy decided suddenly. She should never have come here. It had been ridiculous of her to think for one moment that anything she had to say on this subject would make any impression on Marcus; he was obviously a law unto himself.

He sat forward suddenly, putting his own wineglass down beside hers on the table. 'Danny's right,' he said softly, his narrowed gaze unwavering on her flushed face. 'I have everything to do with his demise from the series.'

Oh, God. Joy briefly closed her eyes. What did she say now?

CHAPTER FIVE

JOY had come here this evening full of outrage that Marcus might have been instrumental in Danny being axed from the series—but now that he had actually confirmed that as fact she was totally speechless. Mainly, she knew, because a part of her had genuinely believed Marcus was incapable of such a petty act.

How did she feel now? Disappointed, mainly; she had hoped that Marcus hadn't been involved.

'More wine?'

'What?' She looked up blankly at Marcus.

He stood with the bottle of wine poised over her glass. 'More wine?' he prompted drily. 'You look as if you could do with some,' he added, as she continued to look dazed.

'Thank you,' she accepted stiffly, no longer looking at him, picking up her refilled glass for something to do—and just as promptly dropping it.

The cooled wine went straight down the front of her jacket to form a pool in the lap of her dress, before being absorbed into that material too.

Joy shot up almost immediately, but it wasn't quickly enough to stop her dress becoming sodden. But, if the truth were known, she would much rather the wine soaked into the dress than into the cream carpet; it looked expensive, and would surely have needed professional cleaning if she had wet it with the wine. Thank God the glass had also landed unharmed on the thick carpet.

She gave Marcus a stricken look. 'I'm sorry——'

'I'll get you a towel,' he rasped, turning on his heel to leave the room.

He looked furious. She knew she had been clumsy, realised it was probably an expensive wine she had spilt, but there had been no real harm done. Except to Lisa's dress. Yet another apology she was going to have to make to the other woman.

Marcus didn't look any more pleased when he returned to the room with the promised towel, his gaze icy, his mouth a thin uncompromising line. 'Here.' He thrust the towel at her.

Joy gave him a frowning look before mopping at her damp dress. The more she mopped, the worse it looked. She had a feeling she was going to owe Lisa more than an apology for this dress—probably a whole month's wages so that the other woman could replace it. If it was replaceable; it was probably one of Lisa's designer gowns, an original, a one-off. Oh, God...!

'It would probably be better if you took it off,' Marcus rasped harshly.

She looked up at him sharply. Take her dress off? With only that tiny pair of briefs underneath? He had to be joking.

'I'll get you a robe,' he added abruptly.

'No!' Joy halted his progress out of the room, standing up straight as he slowly turned to look at her. 'I—I'll go back to the hotel and get changed. I... Perhaps they'll be able to do something with the dress,' she added, with a grimace at the sodden-looking material.

'I doubt it.' Marcus echoed her own sentiments. 'It needs to be done now, the worst of the wine sponged out.'

And she had no intention of taking off her dress in Marcus's apartment. 'If I order a taxi, I can be back at the hotel in a few minutes.' She picked up her handbag.

'I'll drive you back,' Marcus told her coldly, 'if you really insist on going back now.'

Of course she insisted on going back now; she could hardly sit here in this wet dress. Besides, now that Marcus had confirmed he had been involved in Danny being axed, she no longer knew what to say to him.

'We could also conclude our conversation, once you've changed.' Once again he seemed to read her thoughts.

'I thought it was concluded,' she said stiffly.

'Hardly,' he drawled. 'We had barely got started. Before the accident with your wine.'

Joy looked at him sharply. She didn't particularly like the way he had said 'accident'... Surely he didn't think she had deliberately dropped the wine down herself? What possible reason could she have for doing such a thing?

She drew in a ragged breath. 'It was an accident, Marcus——'

'I thought we had already established that?' He arched dark brows. Mockingly, it seemed to Joy.

'*I* know it was an accident, Marcus,' she snapped. 'You're the one who seems to be having some problem accepting that!'

He shrugged. 'You arrive unexpectedly, obviously dressed for an evening out, throw out accusations, and then proceed to spill wine all over yourself—what conclusions am I supposed to draw from that?' he drawled disgustedly.

There was heated colour in Joy's cheeks. 'Not the ones you have obviously drawn!' She glared at him. 'Never mind about ordering the taxi.' She moved determinedly towards the corridor that led to the lift. 'I'll get one once I'm outside.'

'Joy——'

'Don't say another word, Marcus!' She turned on him warningly. 'And, as I told you this morning, maybe you should meet a different crowd of people—perhaps then your thinking might not be as warped as theirs obviously is!' Her head high, her back stiff with indignation, she left the room.

And her heart beat loudly in her chest until the gentle whirring sound heralded the arrival of the lift she had so hastily summoned, all the time half expecting an angry Marcus to have followed her. As she quickly stepped inside, pressing the button for the ground floor, she knew that he hadn't, and was able to breathe more easily again.

How dared he? Just what did he think she was doing by coming to see him in this way? Offering him her body in exchange for the possibility of Danny being given his job back? Considering how cheaply he seemed to think she held her body, she couldn't see how he might think she'd believe he would be swayed by such an offer!

As he hadn't been. Perhaps that was the biggest insult of all; he had been furious at the thought of being duped, and certainly had no interest in following it through. Joy had never felt so humiliated in her life.

So much for her claim that she would get a taxi once she was outside. Taxis just didn't roam the streets in this prestigious part of London, probably because most of the people who lived here had their own transport, or would have rung for a taxi before leaving home. As Joy had intended doing before leaving Marcus's. Before he had insulted her in the way he had.

Oh, well, a walk in the—— Rain. It was raining. On top of everything else that had gone wrong this evening, it was now raining. Lisa's dress—if it wasn't already—was going to be ruined. It was——

'Get in!'

Joy turned sharply to look at the car that had drawn up beside her on the road. A black car, its model difficult to make out in the dim street-lighting. But its driver was all too well known to her.

'No, thank you,' she told Marcus stiffly. 'I prefer to walk.' She would rather catch pneumonia than suffer any more of this man's company.

'I said, get in, Joy,' he bit out tautly, his mood obviously not having improved in the few minutes since they had parted.

'And I said——'

'You're a damned stubborn woman!' Even as he spoke he was getting out of the driver's side of the car to stride forcefully round to where she still stood on the pavement. 'Get in the damned car, Joy, before we both get drowned in this downpour!' His eyes glittered dangerously in the semi-darkness.

He wasn't exaggerating about the force of the rain; it was absolutely pouring down. Joy's hair was hanging in wet tendrils about her face, her jacket was already soaked through. And the dress ... This poor dress would never be the same, she was sure of it.

Her only consolation was that, in the few brief minutes he had been out of the car, Marcus had got almost as wet as she was. But, nevertheless, she still had no intention of accepting a lift from him. He was arrogant, impossible, totally——

'I'm not about to argue with you any more,' he snapped, as he saw the stubborn determination on her face. He opened the passenger door of the car before grasping her arm and bundling her inside, slamming the door firmly behind her before going round the car to get in behind the wheel.

The whole process had taken about thirty seconds to accomplish, and Joy was left reeling in surprise at finding herself suddenly inside the warm comfort of Marcus's car. How had he done that? Before she even had time to formulate a reply to her own question, Marcus had turned on the ignition and directed the car out into the road.

'I don't——'

'No—don't!' He turned very briefly to glare at her. 'I'm really not in the mood to argue with you,' he added grimly.

He wasn't in the mood? He should try putting himself in her place—she had been insulted, and then as good as forced into his car! And, now that she was here, there was no point in arguing about the latter any further. Not that she didn't still have plenty to say about the former. But it could wait until they reached her hotel; at least then she would only have to walk upstairs to her suite, whereas if he threw her out of the car now she might end up walking most of the way back in the rain to the hotel.

If he thought her obedience of silence unusual, he didn't say so, his expression still grim as he manoeuvred the car in and out of the busy London traffic. Not that Joy believed for a minute that the traffic was his problem; that didn't seem to bother him in the least as he drove with ease and competence. No, *she* was his problem. Well, that was OK—because he was hers.

She still couldn't believe his arrogance in assuming she had deliberately spilt that wine down herself, with the sole intention of having to remove her dress and then seducing him. He might think she held her body cheaply, but she certainly didn't, and she wasn't about to trade it for the possibility of Danny Eames's receiving a reprieve from being axed from the television series. Even if Danny had really been a friend of hers, she wouldn't have been preapred to do that.

'We haven't finished our conversation concerning *Pilgrim's Game*,' Marcus began grimly as they approached her hotel.

'Oh, I think we have,' Joy dismissed with a contemptuopus look in his direction. 'More than finished it,' she added disgustedly. As far as she was concerned, there was nothing more to be said on the subject; Marcus had admitted he was the one responsible for Danny being axed and, after his attitude towards her in his apartment, she had no intention of even trying to change his mind. A mind as unrelenting as his couldn't possibly be changed.

'No, I don't think we——'

'Oh, my God!' Joy's interruption had been completely spontaneous. Nothing could have prevented the outburst as her horrified gaze fixed on the events taking place outside her hotel.

Danny Eames was engaged in an argument with the doorman as the other man tried to help him into a waiting taxi, and, from the way Danny was swaying unsteadily on his feet, Joy didn't think he had stayed up in her suite while she had been away. She was sure that he must have returned to the bar to drink even more. But it was the man standing on the other side of Danny, also trying to get him to enter the taxi, who really threw Joy. It was Casey. What was her cousin doing here?

'Don't you think it's time for introductions now, Joy?' Marcus prompted harshly, his gaze fixed on her compellingly as she sat across the room from him.

Joy was still shaken. It had been the biggest shock of her life to arrive back at the hotel to witness the scene she had, and she still hadn't recovered from what had followed.

With expected efficiency Marcus had parked his car behind the taxi, instructing Joy to wait in the car while he went to the aid of the two men still trying unsuccessfully to get the now loudly abusive Danny Eames into the back of the taxi. As soon as he had seen the older man, Danny had become even more verbally offensive, and heated colour had entered Joy's cheeks at some of the language.

But Marcus had seemed immune to it all, taking over from the doorman and Casey, bundling the younger man inside the taxi and firmly closing the door behind him before he could get out again, issuing quick-fire instructions to the waiting driver before handing him some money, obviously intended to cover the fare.

By that time Joy had managed to climb out of Marcus's car, although on slightly shaky legs, and she had waited with some trepidation as the three men left standing on the pavement had given themselves a congratulatory pat on the back for a job well done.

But, the doorman back in his position outside the main hotel door, Marcus and Casey had been left looking at each other, until, that was, Casey had spotted Joy standing beside Marcus's car. Her cousin had given a whoop of delight as he had hurried over to give her one of his usual bear-hugs.

All Joy had been able to think at that particular moment was, what a *mess*.

She still had no idea what Casey was doing here in London, but with the three of them standing there on the pavement looking at each other, the two men—Marcus in particular—with speculation, she had had no choice but to suggest that they all retired upstairs to her suite.

Which was where they were now. And Marcus wanted an introduction to Casey. Who couldn't be Casey. Because she was—supposedly—Casey Simms. What a *mess*!

'Marcus Ballantyne,' she told Casey stiltedly, desperately trying to catch her cousin's eye as his mouth fell open at the confirmation of what he had obviously already suspected. 'And this is Charles Simms,' she introduced with a firmness that had her cousin's head whipping round as he looked at her with puzzlement, obviously wondering what she was doing using his middle name for the introduction.

'Any relation?' Marcus rasped, after briefly— very briefly—shaking the younger man by the hand, once again looking at Joy with those compelling blue eyes.

Casey was still dumbstruck by the identity of the other man, and so it was left to Joy to answer him. But she could see by Marcus's expression that he suspected Casey might be the 'husband' she had left at home so that she could come to London to have a good time with a number of male friends. Damn nerve!

'My cousin,' she snapped, returning Marcus's gaze challengingly.

He held that gaze for several long seconds before turning back to look at Casey. By this time Casey had completely recovered from the shock of meeting the other man, grinning at Marcus in his usual friendly manner. But the grin faltered slightly as Marcus remained unsmiling.

'I can't see any family resemblance,' Marcus finally said softly.

There wasn't any; Joy freely admitted that. She and Casey looked absolutely nothing alike, their colouring completely different, their builds certainly so. Casey was almost as big and powerful-looking as Marcus. But that didn't alter the fact that they were cousins—more like brother and

sister, really—and she didn't like Marcus's implication that it could be otherwise.

She shrugged dismissively. 'Nevertheless, it's a
fact,' she told him offhandedly. She had no intention of justifying her claim by explaining that,
although Casey's father and her own were brothers,
her father had married a red-haired Irish girl, while
Casey's father had married a beautiful Italian girl
he had met while holidaying there. That was really
none of Marcus's business.

'You really are *the* Marcus Ballantyne, aren't
you?' Casey was still staring at the other man, the
question of him being referred to as Charles an unimportant one for the moment, as far as he was
concerned. 'The actor,' he added unnecessarily.

Marcus nodded abrupt confirmation of the fact,
his expression still grim. 'I really am,' he said uninterestedly. 'What exactly happened here earlier?'
He looked at the younger man with narrowed eyes.

The brief introductions over, Marcus had gone
straight back to what he really wanted to know.
And, in all honestly, Joy was curious to know too.
How on earth had Casey and Danny ever got
together in the first place, let alone embroiled in
that scene outside?

Marcus's icy gaze flickered over her. 'Why don't
you go and change out of that damp dress while
your...cousin and I talk?' he suggested evenly.

Only it wasn't a suggestion, as far as Joy was
concerned; it sounded more like an order. And this
man was far too fond of issuing orders—and expecting them to be obeyed. And she hadn't missed
the slight hesitation in Marcus's voice before he referred to Casey as her cousin. Although she had to

admit the dress was still damp and very uncomfortable to wear. But if she left these two men alone for any length of time...

Casey was looking at her curiously now. 'What happened to the dress?'

She knew she could have claimed it had got wet in the rain, and that was partially true; the rain certainly hadn't improved its condition. But she and Marcus both knew that wasn't the reason the dress was probably ruined.

'I spilt some wine down it earlier——'

'Thank God for that,' her cousin said with some relief, grinning at her as she looked at him with raised brows. 'I smelt the wine on you earlier, and thought you had gone completely off the rails!'

Wonderful—her cousin had thought he had *two* drunks to deal with in one evening. 'I'll only be a couple of minutes,' she told them firmly. 'If you would care to wait before giving the explanations, Ca—— Charles.' She gave an impatient sigh as she almost slipped up on the confusion of the names. Tangled webs!

'Sure.' Casey shrugged before throwing himself down into one of the armchairs. He looked up at the older man. 'I would offer you a drink while we're waiting, but I think Danny Eames more or less cleared the minibar out.'

So that was where Danny had got the additional alcohol, Joy realised as she went into the bedroom to change. She had completely forgotten about that little fridge-bar in the corner of the lounge, probably because she knew she had no intention of using it. But Danny had obviously discovered it all too easily.

She wasted no time on further thought, about Danny or anything else, quickly pulling on the pair of jeans and the black jumper she had been wearing earlier; she didn't want to give Casey and Marcus too much time to talk, and certainly didn't want the forthright Casey asking too many questions without her in the room. Or Marcus either, for that matter, because she was sure he didn't believe her explanation of Casey being her cousin.

The two men were talking about *Pilgrim's Game* as she came back into the room, reminding Joy all too forcefully of the reason she had gone to see Marcus at all this evening. Her resolve hardened as she remembered his admission concerning Danny.

Marcus turned to look at her. He was seated opposite Casey now. The two men were of similar build and colouring, but there the similarity ended. Casey had an open and honest face, his eyes always full of laughter, whereas the years had etched lines and experience and cynicism on Marcus's face, and those blue eyes were usually guarded. As they were now...

'I've ordered coffee for us all,' he informed her dismissively now.

Of course he had. Marcus seemed to have a habit of taking over, wherever he might be. The fact that it was her suite, and her hotel bill, was totally irrelevant to him!

'So?' Casey turned to her eagerly, semingly unaware of the tension that existed between Joy and Marcus. 'I'm still waiting to hear all the lurid details, Joy.' He grinned at her encouragingly.

That was his reason for being here, she was well aware of that. She had been less than forthcoming on the telephone earlier and, being the impulsive Casey that he was, he had decided to come here and see for himself what she was up to. Well, she wasn't up to anything. Although on the evidence he had seen so far—first Danny in her hotel suite, and then her arrival back with Marcus—she somehow didn't think Casey was going to believe that.

'I think we all are,' Marcus drawled harshly.

She shrugged, deliberately not looking at Marcus but turning to Casey. 'When did you arrive?'

'When your friend Danny was on his fourth mini-bottle of whisky, I think,' Casey said with amusement. 'The people in Reception seemed to think you were in your suite, because you hadn't handed in your key but when I knocked on the door Danny Eames was the one to open it. Obviously the worse for wear,' he added ruefully.

'Seriously so,' Marcus put in gratingly.

Joy still kept her head averted so that she couldn't see the disapproval on his face. 'That still doesn't explain how the two of you ended up in the street,' she prompted softly.

Casey shrugged. 'He started throwing punches almost as soon as he opened the door.' He glanced at Marcus speculatively. 'He seemed to think I was you . . .?'

'I don't doubt it,' Marcus acknowledged drily.

'But the two of you work together.' Casey was obviously puzzled. 'You haven't been causing trouble between the two of them, have you, Joy?' her cousin added teasingly.

And now was definitely not the time for his impish sense of humour to come into play. Casey had been teasing her all her life, and for the main part she enjoyed it, but not now!

'Certainly not,' she snapped dismissively— although she still wasn't altogether sure whether or not that was true. Marcus had admitted being instrumental in Danny's dismissal from the series. But surely that could have nothing to do with her...?

Casey gave a disbelieving snort. 'Well, anyway, Eames was way out of line, totally drunk, so I just frog-marched him down in the lift and out of the hotel. Unfortunately the fresh air had a disastrous effect on him, and he started swinging the punches again. Incidentally, the doorman may have a black eye in the morning.' He frowned. 'The poor chap walked straight into a well-aimed left hook.'

This was all so much worse than Joy had even imagined. She wouldn't be surprised if the management asked her to leave after this evening's events. After all, Danny had remained here as her guest while she went out—only because she had thought her suite was the safest place to leave him in his condition, but she doubted the hotel management would be too impressed with that explanation.

'I'll deal with that before I leave,' Marcus put in quietly.

Joy gave him a sharp look. She didn't doubt that he could deal with it, she just couldn't help wondering why, feeling about Danny as he obviously did, he would want to bother.

'I know I said go away and have some fun, Joy, live a little——' Casey was grinning at her again '—but I certainly didn't expect this!'

Neither had she. And she didn't appreciate Casey's amusement at her expense, either. He had to know she was hating every minute of this.

'Very funny, C—— Charles.' Damn, she really would have to try and remember that, for the moment, in Marcus's presence, he wasn't Casey. 'I've had a disastrous time, and you think it's hilarious!' she said disgustedly.

'Oh, come on, Joy,' her cousin chided lightly. 'No woman can be having a disastrous time when two men are fighting over her.'

Casey thought Danny had mistaken him for Marcus and started swinging at him in a drunken rage because both men were interested in her! If he had known Danny for any length of time—in a sober state—Casey would have quickly realised that the only person Danny Eames was interested in was Danny Eames. And as for Marcus...!

'I doubt if Marcus appreciates the implication that he would have to fight for any woman,' she said scathingly. 'And I certainly——' She broke off as there was a knock on the door.

'Saved by the coffee,' Casey said with amusement, before standing up to go to the door.

Joy was suddenly very aware of being alone with Marcus. Not that she was really, with Casey only a few feet away answering the door, but it felt as if the two of them were alone in the room. And she felt very uncomfortable, knowing Marcus was looking at her with those speculative eyes. He hadn't believed the explanation of Casey being her cousin, and she freely acknowledgd that nothing that had been said since then had been guaranteed to convince him of it.

But she didn't have to convince him of anything. She hadn't even known him until yesterday—was it only yesterday?—and she owed him no explanations concerning anything in her life. Although she had to admit Casey turning up in this way did look rather suspect...

'You certainly...?' Marcus prompted softly from across the room.

She looked over at him sharply, her brow clearing as she realised he wanted her to finish what she had been saying. 'I would not enjoy the experience of having two men fight over me,' she told him firmly.

Marcus raised dark brows. 'You prefer more than that number?'

Joy drew in an angry breath. 'I don't——'

'Just joking, Joy,' he cut in drily, his mouth twisted ruefully. 'Somewhere among all this confusion we seem to have lost our sense of humour.'

By 'we', she knew he meant her. But she couldn't find anything in the least humorous about this situation—and she didn't think he did either.

'Coffee.' Casey put the laden tray down on the low table in the middle of the room. 'Do you want to be mother, Joy?' he suggested mockingly.

She wanted both of them to leave, wanted to go to bed, bury her head beneath the covers—and hope all this had been a terrible nightmare. It was the last time, positively the last time, that she would ever let Casey persuade her into doing anything!

'Not particularly,' she snapped irritably.

Casey began to pour the coffee himself, not in the least perturbed by her mood. 'And I always thought you wanted children?' he teased as he handed her the full cup of coffee.

She had wanted children. With Gerald. She had secretly dreamed of the day they would marry and begin a family together. She had believed Gerald, with his calm maturity, would make a wonderful father. Her dreams had been sandcastles, which, when the tide came in, were completely obliterated...

'Just pour the coffee, Charles,' she bit out forcefully.

Casey raised knowing brows as he turned back to Marcus. 'PMT can be hell to live with,' he muttered wryly.

'And don't be so damned patronising.' Joy's eyes flashed warningly.

Casey raised his eyes heavenwards. 'You see what I mean?' He grimaced in Marcus's direction.

'I don't have PMT, I simply have a case of Londonitis! The place is making me ill!' she explained abruptly, as both men looked puzzled.

Marcus gave a slight inclination of his head. 'It can be...wearing on the nerves,' he drawled.

Epecially if you have several men in attendance at the same time, his tone implied. Well...to Joy, it seemed to imply that. Or maybe she was just becoming over-sensitive to the whole situation. Although she didn't think so. Marcus had made his opinion of her more than clear earlier, and certainly nothing that had happened since could have improved on that.

'That's putting it mildly,' she agreed gratingly. 'Look, I don't know about you two, but I, for one have had enough for one evening, and would like to get to bed.' She just wanted them both to leave; she felt as if she couldn't take any more. Marcus she didn't want to see again, and Casey she could sort out once she was back home. Right now she just wanted some peace. And space.

Marcus glanced across at Casey. 'Don't mind us...' he told Joy softly.

Casey met the other man's glance, a mischievous glint in his eyes. 'No, don't mind us at all, Joy,' he echoed lightly.

She looked at the two of them with frustrated anger. If either of them thought she was going to leave the two of them alone here together, they were mistaken—she had more sense than that. 'Where are you staying tonight, Charles?' She looked pointedly at Casey.

He returned her gaze innocently. 'Why, here, of course—Joy,' he returned pointedly—letting Joy know that he had finally caught on to the reason she kept calling him Charles, and that he was enjoying her discomfort over the whole situation.

It was so typically Casey that she couldn't even be annoyed with him. But she did intend bringing this evening to a close as quickly as possible. Otherwise she knew Casey would play on the situation for all he was worth; it would appeal to his warped sense of humour.

'Here?' she repeated with a frown.

Casey raised dark brows at her surprise. 'It will be far from the first time we've slept together,' he said drily.

It might be, but the last time it had actually happened she had been eight years old and Casey had been eleven. Although she could see by the sudden hardness of Marcus's expression, and the cold glint in his eyes, that he had a completely different impression.

'Kissing-cousins, hmm?' he said coldly, sitting forward to put his empty coffee-cup down on the table before standing up. 'In that case, I'll leave you to it.'

'It' being she and Casey going to bed together. God, this was ridiculous. How had she, in the course of two days, suddenly become such a *femme fatale*? In Marcus's eyes anyway. What made it all so much more ludicrous was that she was a twenty-seven-year-old virgin!

It had bothered her sometimes that Gerald hadn't tried to push their relationship on to a more intimate level. After all, four years of seeing each other almost every day was a long time. But she had decided that, with his old-fashioned views, he had just been waiting until they were married before they began a physical relationship. When he had ended their relationship so suddenly, she had taken an altogether different view, and had decided that she just hadn't been physically attractive to him. It had made her wonder whether she was physically attractive to anyone...

But her time in Marcus's arms earlier today had made a mockery of that idea. Marcus had found her very attractive; he would have made love to her if Casey's telephone call hadn't interrupted them.

'Goodbye, Joy.' He stood at the door now, ready to leave, so tall and dark and powerful.

She looked at him dazedly, lost in her memories of her time earlier today in his arms. On this very couch. And now he was leaving. And she would never see him again.

Why did she suddenly have a heavy feeling in her chest at the thought of that happening?'

'I need hardly say, enjoy the rest of your stay in London,' he added gratingly, his eyes glacial.

As far as Joy was concerned, this was the last of her stay in London; she intended returning home with Casey when he left in the morning.

'Nice to meet you, Marcus.' Casey had joined the other man at the door, holding out his hand for Marcus to shake.

Marcus nodded abruptly, returning the other man's gesture. 'Joy.' He nodded again, in her direction this time.

And then he was gone, and Casey was closing the door behind him. Joy hadn't moved, sitting motionless on the sofa.

'Now...' Casey turned back to her determinedly. 'Would you like to tell me how you ended up with a drunken Danny Eames in your hotel suite—and a furious Marcus Ballantyne in your heart?'

His words hit Joy like a hammer-blow. And she promptly burst into tears.

CHAPTER SIX

'How was your first day back at the library?' Casey sat, as he usually did, on top of one of the worktops in Joy's kitchen.

Her first day back at the library had been eventful, to say the least.

She had returned to her flat briefly, after coming back from London with Casey, but only really for long enough to pick up some of her own clothes before driving down to visit her parents for the rest of her holiday. They had been pleased to see her, as they always were, and it had been a few days of relative peace after what had seemed like madness.

It had been a time when she had sat and reflected on her life, taken stock—and come to the conclusion that Casey was right; she really couldn't continue to work at the library, with Gerald, any longer.

It wasn't going to be easy finding another job, she appreciated that, but continuing as she was wasn't easy either. And, after her time in London, she knew she couldn't continue to waste her life any longer. And she was wasting it. She knew she had to move on. If being in London hadn't given her the fun and excitement, the 'living a little' that Casey had hoped for, it had at least given her that.

Gerald's reaction, after reading her letter of resignation, had come as a surprise. He had been totally shocked, searching her out as she worked to invite her to his office so that they could talk about it.

There had been nothing to talk about, as far as Joy was concerned; her mind was made up. It had taken her six months to reach this point in her life, and a traumatic few days in London, but her mind *was* made up. As she had told Gerald.

'Well?' Casey prompted again now, having arrived at her flat shortly after she got in from work. 'Don't tell me,' he grinned, at her lack of response. 'Gerald missed you so much this last week that he swept you up into his arms as soon as he saw you and declared undying love!' His eyes danced with mischief at the very idea.

Joy frowned, heated colour entering her cheeks. In truth, Gerald had used every other persuasion but that one to try and get her to withdraw her resignation. 'Don't be ridiculous, Casey,' she snapped irritably.

'Well, something's wrong.' He was looking at her frowningly now, trying to assess the situation. And failing. 'Marcus has telephoned you and declared undying love?' he said hopefully.

As quickly as the colour had entered her cheeks it now drained away. She and Casey hadn't discussed Marcus at all since Casey had come out with that outrageous remark in her hotel suite after Marcus's departure, her cousin seeming to realise he had more than touched on a raw nerve. After she had burst into tears in that way, that wasn't surprising.

She wasn't even sure why she had reacted in that way. Marcus certainly hadn't been 'in her heart' then; she had hardly even known him, so how could

he have been? But even so, he had touched something inside her, evoked a physical response she had
never known before. A response that even now
threw her into confusion.

But at the same time she knew it was her meeting
with him that had helped her decide that she had
to move on in her life. Because her reaction to him
had at least shown her that, inside, she had already
moved on; it was just a question of physically doing
so now. Hence the handing in of her notice. She
had no idea what she was going to do careerwise
instead; she just knew that continuing to work with
Gerald in this way was holding her back in all ways.

'Now you're being even more ridiculous, Casey,'
she told him impatiently. 'And will you move out
of the way so that I can finish cooking our meal?'
She looked at him pointedly until he climbed down
off her worktop.

'But you haven't talked about Marcus at all.' He
continued to look at her curiously.

'Because there's nothing to tell,' she said briskly,
moving efficiently about the kitchen, putting the
finishing touches to the spaghetti bolognese she was
making for the two of them. Lisa was once again
working this evening and, as usual when Casey was
at a loose end, he had arrived on Joy's doorstep
expecting her to cook a meal for him.

'No?'

'Casey...'

'Yes?' He looked down at her with those widely
innocent blue eyes.

Joy gave an impatient sigh. She had known this
would come, of course; it wasn't like Casey to be
tactful for long. In fact, if she hadn't gone to see

her parents for a few days, she had no doubt this conversation would have taken place long ago. Nevertheless, she still wasn't ready for it. She had tried not to think about her time with Marcus, knew she couldn't rationalise it. It had existed—but now it was over.

'No,' she told Casey flatly.

He gave a disappointed sigh. 'You're no fun, Joy!'

She gave a self-derisive smile. 'I think I had all the fun I need during those few days in London.'

'You never did tell me——'

'And I'm not about to either,' she interrupted firmly. 'Now, make yourself useful, Casey, and lay the table.'

He raised dark brows. 'End of subject?'

'End of subject,' she nodded.

'Your secret, hmm?' He grimaced.

'There is no——' She broke off as her doorbell rang. 'Go and answer that for me, will you?' She sighed her impatience. 'Whoever it is, we're about to have dinner,' she reminded him as he went to the door.

She could hear the murmur of voices in the other room, and wondered who on earth could be calling on her at this time of the evening. Unless Lisa had finished early, and also wanted dinner? Oh, well, there was enough food here for the three of them if that was the case.

'A visitor for you, Joy,' Casey said softly behind her.

His tone of voice made her turn to him with a frown, the questioning speculation of his expression not encouraging either. 'Who is it?' she said warily.

Casey pursed his lips thoughtfully. 'Why don't you go in the other room and find out for yourself?' he suggested lightly.

Joy didn't like the way he was looking at her. Just who was this visitor? Obviously Casey wasn't about to tell her, so she would have to go and find out for herslf.

Gerald!

She only just stopped her mouth dropping open in the surprise of seeing him here. He hadn't been to her flat since the evening he had told her so apologetically that he had decided to end their relationship, so that he could go out with the attractive widow. He had seemed to consider he was behaving rightly and properly. After a four-year relationship between the two of them, Joy hadn't agreed with him. She still didn't.

'Good evening, Gerald,' she greeted him coolly, quickly recovering from the shock of his being here at all. 'What can I do for you?'

Gerald was tall and slightly stooped, his mousy-brown hair styled back from his face to show his slightly receding hairline. It was difficult for Joy not to compare him with Marcus Ballantyne—and to find Gerald very much wanting when it came to looks. Oh, she knew looks weren't that important, appreciated that the personality of a person was what counted, and that she hadn't liked Marcus's admission of being instrumental in having Danny Eames removed from *Pilgrim's Game*, but then, she hadn't particularly liked Gerald's behaviour six months ago either.

Gerald glanced towards the kitchen. 'I see your cousin still spends as much time here.'

Casey's familiarity with—and frequent visits to— her home had always been a bone of contention between Gerald and herself. He had never understood the close bond that existed between herself and Casey, considering it strange that a male cousin should want to spend so much time with her. Joy had given up trying to explain the closeness to him—and she certainly didn't welcome the implied criticism now.

'We were just about to have dinner, Gerald, so unless it's something important...?' She looked at him pointedly.

She had once loved this man, had wanted to marry him, to have his children—and yet, looking at him now, he was just a middle-aged man, slightly too thin for his height, with thinning hair, and only a mildly attractive face. A stranger, in fact.

He shifted uncomfortably, sensing that her mood was not welcoming. Well, what had he expected? He had left her private life six months ago, had treated her extremely distantly at work ever since, something she had found very difficult to deal with; he couldn't now expect to arrive at her home and be given the red-carpet treatment. If he did, then he was even less sensitive than she had given him credit for.

He looked at her frowningly with rather hurt brown eyes. 'I thought we could talk, Joy,' he said softly.

She met his gaze unflinchingly. 'Concerning what?'

'You handed in your notice today——'

'You didn't?' A stunned Casey had emerged from the kitchen—where Joy knew he had been avidly listening to every word of the conversation taking place in the sitting-room. She had thought Casey's curiosity would be sure to get the better of him so that he couldn't resist eavesdropping. And it had.

She turned to give him a mockingly reproving look. 'Yes, I did,' she assured him mildly.

'Well, good for you!' He grinned his approval. 'About time, too.'

She was only too aware of Casey's opinion of her staying on at the library and working with Gerald once their relationship was over. 'Some of us take a little longer than others to realise what's the right thing to do,' she told him derisively. 'That isn't to say we don't get there in the end.'

Casey raised his brows. 'This wouldn't have anything to do with what happened in London, would it?'

'London?' Gerald echoed in a puzzled voice. 'But I thought you went to visit your parents for the week, Joy?'

She had told him that when she had put the request in for the week's holiday, because, quite frankly, she didn't think it was any of his business what she was really doing; she certainly hadn't wanted him to know she was going away to London for the week because Casey had won the trip as first prize in a competition and he didn't want to go. She did have some pride.

She met Gerald's gaze calmly. 'I did for part of the week. But I also spent several days in London.' She shrugged dismissively. 'It really isn't important where I spent the time, Gerald,' she added offhandedly, deliberately not looking at Casey, who, she knew, thought the time she had spent in London was very important.

'Do you have a job there, is that it?' Gerald frowned disapprovingly. 'Because running away doesn't help, you know, Joy.'

'And just how would you know?' Casey was the one to challenge him. 'Besides, Joy has never run away from anything in her life,' he added indignantly.

Thank you, Casey, Joy thought gratefully, outraged that Gerald could even think of suggesting she was running away—the damned nerve! If she had been going to do that, she would have done it months ago, not now. It had just taken her until now, after her time spent in London, to realise she had to get on with her life.

'Just accept my resignation, Gerald,' she told him wearily. 'It will be easier for everyone if you do.'

'But——'

'Aren't you listening, Gerald?' Casey cut in firmly. 'Joy has decided to leave. It isn't for you to try and talk her out of it.'

'As her superior, I beg to differ,' Gerald told him stiffly.

'I don't happen to consider you superior to Joy in any way,' Casey bit out scornfully. 'On the contrary!' he added scathingly.

There had never been any love lost between the two men and, since the relationship between Joy and Gerald had ended, Casey had made no secret of his view of the other man. But, even so, Joy didn't particularly want a full-scale argument between the two of them in her home.

'You know very well what I mean, Simms,' Gerald snapped irritably. 'Joy is a wonderful worker. The library will be sorry to see her go.'

'The library can damn well learn to do without her,' Casey scorned. 'I'm just grateful she's at last seen the light.'

'But——'

'I really think it would be best if you left, Gerald,' Joy cut in firmly. 'Casey and I were just about to eat our dinner,' she added again pointedly.

'And you aren't invited,' Casey rasped insultingly.

'Casey!' she reproved softly, giving him a warning look before turning back to Gerald. 'We can talk about this again at work tomorrow. If you think it necessary.' Her tone implied that she didn't consider it was; she had made her mind up. She wasn't about to change it again, no matter what the persuasion to do otherwise.

She didn't really know why Gerald was bothering. It had been difficult for both of them to continue working together in the way that they had, after what had happened. She would have thought Gerald would be as relieved as she felt. Still, after the way he had shocked her by ending their relationship in the first place, she didn't even try to understand the way he thought any more.

Gerald was stiffly indignant after Casey's rudeness to him. 'I think it is,' he told her abruptly. 'Come to my office as soon as you get in tomorrow.' He turned to leave.

'Goodbye to you too!' Casey muttered when Joy returned from seeing Gerald to the door.

'You weren't exactly polite to him, either, Casey,' she pointed out lightly.

Casey looked thoughtful, his eyes narrowed. 'I wonder what's really eating him?' he finally murmured softly.

Joy gave him a sharp look. 'What do you mean?'

'Just watch him, Joy, that's all,' Casey warned as he followed her back into the kitchen. 'I always thought there was something dog-in-the-manger about him.'

She didn't even pretend to know what Casey was talking about, had no interest in Gerald or his motives, quickly grabbing the spaghetti off the hotplate before it was spoilt completely. She was a little surprised at Gerald for coming here, she had to admit, but it made no difference to her decision. She was going to leave the library once she had worked her month's notice, whether she had another job or not.

It was amazing the feeling of freedom having made that decision gave her...

Watching Marcus and Danny in *Pilgrim's Game* no one would ever have guessed at the real feelings that existed between the two men; they gave every impression of being totally in tune with each other. Of course it was acting, and there was no doubting Marcus's ability to do that, but, nevertheless, it was strange to sit watching the two men on the television screen, and know that they actually disliked each other intensely.

Joy wasn't even sure what had made her watch the programme; she rarely had in the past. But she hadn't been able to resist the impulse to turn on the television at the time she knew *Pilgrim's Game* was on.

There was no doubting Marcus's charisma, even on the television screen; he had about him such an air of powerful attraction he was almost magnetic to watch. Joy couldn't take her eyes off him, anyway.

To think she had spent time with this man, been held in his arms, been kissed by him until she was almost senseless. Almost? She had been senseless! What other explanation could she give for almost having made love with a man she hadn't known for even twenty-four hours?

Gerald had tried again over the past few days to persuade her to withdraw her resignation. Why, she had no idea. All she did know was that she had remained adamant. She had to. It was time to move on in her life.

Where, she wasn't sure. The job prospects didn't look too good so far. But she remained hopeful. And Casey had been—for once—a tremendous help. So positive. It wasn't actually like Casey to be so helpful, but for the moment she would give him the benefit of the doubt...

Her attention returned to the screen. She had lost the gist of the story completely, her attention all on the man who dominated the programme. And he had believed she was nothing but a spoilt rich wife, in London for some fun. Incredible—she wasn't any of those things. Or ever likely to be, either.

She frowned her irritation as the doorbell rang. It was almost nine o'clock at night. Casey! And he had forgotten his key too. He had never had any consideration for anyone else. Why was it that she loved him so much?

'Case——' Her exasperated greeting froze in her throat as she stared at the man who stood outside her door. Marcus! After so recently watching him on the television screen, it was even more of a shock to see him standing here in the flesh—so to speak. Colour warmed her cheeks as she realised where her thoughts had taken her. 'Marcus...' she greeted him lamely.

He was dressed in blue this time, a dark blue silk shirt and dark blue corduroys, with a dark blue jacket. All of them the colour of his eyes...

'Joy,' he returned huskily.

She was recovering quickly from her shock. And, as she did so, one thought screamed inside her head: what was he doing here?

And then other thoughts tumbled on top of that one. How had he found out where she lived? Why had he bothered to find out?

'Can I come in?' he drawled, at her continued silence.

Could he? For what purpose? What was the point of his being here at all? Hadn't they made their feelings towards each other perfectly obvious last week?

'Joy?' he prompted softly.

Her flat was a mess. She had been in the process of sorting out her clothes before she had been tempted to sit down to watch *Pilgrim's Game*. Something else her trip to London had shown her— she had actually liked wearing Lisa's clothes, and had decided to go through her wardrobe, throw out what she didn't want, and then buy herself a whole new set of clothes. The new Joy, she had decided. Time to move on in more ways than one!

Consequently, her flat looked more like a jumble sale than the orderly home it normally did. There were piles of clothes on the chairs, as she had been deciding what to keep and what to throw away. And Marcus wanted to come into the mess of that. Not that he realised he would be faced with a mess—but she did.

'Excuse the mess,' she said lamely as she stepped back to allow him through the door. 'I'm having a spring-clean.' That had to be an understatement!

Marcus arched dark brows as he walked past her into the flat. 'A little early, aren't you?' he drawled mockingly.

A little late would better have described the chaos in her sitting-room; some of the clothes strewn about there she had owned for years, and they should have been thrown out long ago. Strange—she really hadn't realised the rut she had fallen into the last four years: the way she dressed, as well as the way she lived her life. In the past she had always dressed to please Gerald, and as his tastes were rather conservative, to say the least...

'Does someone else live with you?' Marcus had picked up some of the clothes she had put out for giving away, frowning at the dowdy style of the brown corduroy skirt he still held in his hand.

Dowdy. That just about described most of her wardrobe to date. Well, all that was about to change. But not until after she had found out what Marcus was doing here.

She took the skirt out of his hand, pushing the rest of the clothes on the floor too, so that he could sit down. 'No,' she answered him abruptly. 'I just don't happen to have had a sort-out for years.' She moved to switch the television off, very conscious of the fact that he must have realised she had been watching *Pilgrim's Game*. 'What can I do for you, Marcus?' She faced him awkwardly across the room, loath to sit down herself, feeling more at an advantage standing up.

However, she was very conscious of the fact that she was still wearing the dark green skirt and jumper that she had worn for work, and that her hair, which had been secured at her nape as usual during the day, was now loosely curling about her face in whispy tendrils after her earlier exertions.

Well, this was the real her. Or, at least, it had been. All that was going to change in future.

Marcus had raised his brows after her last question. 'I would love a cup of coffee—as you're asking,' he drawled wryly.

That wasn't exactly what she had meant. And he knew it.

'And I promise not to spill it down myself,' he added softly, looking across at her expectantly.

And he wasn't disappointed; angry colour instantly darkened Joy's cheeks. 'I told you the wine was an accident——'

Marcus chuckled softly. 'You're very easy to tease.' He smiled at her, a roguish smile, blue eyes warm.

Because she wasn't used to it. Except from Casey. And she just told him to shut up when she had had enough. Marcus wasn't quite the same. Not the same at all . . .

'How did you find me, Marcus?' she asked stiltedly.

'I've had quite a drive, Joy; why don't we have the coffee and talk afterwards, hmm?' he suggested lightly.

Talk about what? she wondered, as she moved about the kitchen preparing the coffee, not the instant that she usually had when she was on her own but the percolated kind that she was sure Marcus was used to. But then, he was used to so much else that she wasn't . . .

Why did that thought give her such a heavy feeling in her chest?

'Coffee,' she said tersely, when she went back into the sitting-room.

Marcus was glancing at the newspaper she had bought earlier that day, but he put it down as soon as she entered the room, moving things aside on the table so that she could put the tray down.

'This is a nice flat,' he said appreciatively as Joy poured the coffee.

'It's home,' she said abruptly. 'You still haven't told me how you found me, Marcus,' she reminded him pointedly, once they had their coffee. She knew she had never mentioned where she lived, and her curiosity had got the better of her.

'The hotel.' He shrugged dismissively.

And she hadn't thought hotels revealed addresses of their guests to just anyone who cared to ask. But then, he wasn't just anyone, he was Marcus Ballantyne, and Joy had a feeling it might not have been a case of who or what you knew, but of who you *were*. And who could resist this man when he turned on the charm?

'Why?' She eyed him warily.

'I asked.' He shrugged again.

Joy gave an impatient sigh. 'No, I meant——'

'I know what you meant, Joy,' Marcus cut in firmly. 'I wanted to see you again.'

'Why?'

His mouth quirked. 'You're starting to sound repetitive.'

Her eyes flashed deeply green. 'And you're being deliberately obtuse! Marcus, what are you doing here?' she said exasperatedly.

He looked at her for several long, lingering moments, seeming to take in everything about her appearance. Joy put a hand up self-consciously to her hair, pushing back several of the loose silky tendrils, aware that, after a day at work, her face was completely bare of make-up. She looked as much of a mess as her flat.

'We have unfinished business,' he finally said harshly.

The only unfinished business she was aware they had was the time she had spent in his arms—and she certainly had no intention of finishing that! 'I don't think so.' She shook her head. What did he think she was? Did he really believe she was a woman who had a string of lovers? And did he want to be one of them?

He stood up abruptly, moving determinedly towards her. 'I want you, Joy.' He spoke almost angrily, standing directly in front of her now.

She swallowed hard. There was no mistaking what he was saying, but——

'I've tried to put you out of my mind——' he shook his head '—but it just isn't possible. I want you. And I intend to have you. Exclusively,' he added grimly.

Joy stared up at him. He didn't want to be *one* of her lovers, he wanted to be *the* one—and the *only* one!

CHAPTER SEVEN

HE COULDN'T be serious!

She had spent the last few days inwardly denying Casey's outrageous statement at the hotel in London, and rationalising her reaction towards Marcus. He was a larger than life figure, in more ways than one, was darkly attractive in a challenging way, while at the same time being a famous personality. No wonder she had been swept off her feet by the attention he had shown towards her. But he certainly wasn't 'in her heart', as Casey had said.

Oh, she had rationalised it like mad, made excuses for her uninhibited attraction towards him, finally deciding that her uncharacteristic behaviour was partly reaction to her disappointment concerning her relationship with Gerald. It had all made so much sense while she was at her parents' house.

But with Marcus standing in the room with her, so tall, and dark, and powerfully attractive, exuding that aura of sensual magnetism she had found it impossible to resist in London, it wasn't so easy to dismiss her response to him. Especially when he was telling her he felt the same attraction towards her.

How could he? She was a dowdy librarian—at least, for another four weeks she was. She didn't live a glamorous life by any means; she worked to support herself and her social life consisted of the occasional dinner out or going to the cinema with friends. It wasn't exciting, by any stretch of the imagination. How could Marcus be attracted to her?

Because he didn't really know her. He had seen someone else in London, a different Joy Simms— because she was supposed to be Casey Simms, in London for frivolous fun and enjoyment. But even though she might now have decided it was time to shake her life up a little, that wasn't who she really was, and no amount of change was going to make her into the glamorous, fun-loving flirt he had assumed her to be.

'Marcus, you don't even know me.' She shook her head, sure that if he had come to know the real her in London, this meeting would never have taken place. 'You believe I'm married, for one thing,' she reminded him indignantly.

'And are you?' he said huskily.

'No!' she said exasperatedly.

'Good,' he returned dismissively.

Joy stared up at him, could feel herself starting to drown in the dark sensuality of those blue eyes. And she couldn't allow that to happen. She might feel attracted to him, but the little she knew about him she didn't particularly like. He had admitted that he had been instrumental in Danny being taken out of *Pilgrim's Game* and, from the timing of that, and Marcus's claim that he wanted her in his life, she could now only assume that had had something to do with her supposed friendship with the other man. That was the act of a man who knew he had the power, and used it, and that didn't endear Marcus to Joy at all.

Then why was her pulse racing, her breathing shallow, her legs starting to shake, as his hands reached out to clasp her upper arms, drawing her slowly towards him?

'I want to know you very much, Joy,' he murmured gruffly, his lips only inches from hers now. 'In every way.'

Joy knew that if he kissed her she would be lost. But in truth she couldn't pull away. She simply didn't have the will. Or the strength. She couldn't allow him to kiss her. She——

As his mouth gently claimed hers she felt her legs buckle completely beneath her, knew she was only stopped from falling to the carpeted floor by the iron strength of his arms about her waist as he moulded her body against his.

It was like drowning; her only thought was to cling on to him, the powerful width of his shoulders, to stop herself from sinking.

His lips moved softly, probingly, against hers, the tip of his tongue rubbing against the moistness of her lips until they parted to allow him entry, his tongue now moving sensually over her teeth, before dipping into the darkness beneath.

The length of her body was curved against his, making her fully aware of his arousal, the warm strength of his desire, and as his hands moved caressingly over the length of her spine Joy could feel her body moulding even closer against his.

She couldn't stop this even if she wanted to. And at this moment she didn't want to; she wanted all the pleasure Marcus had shown her in London, wanted again that singing warmth of desire. And this time she didn't want it to end. Once. Just once, she wanted to know the pleasure of this man. The man she knew she was learning to love——

No! She couldn't love a man like this, a man who used his power to control other people's lives to suit himself. She couldn't fall in love with a man like that!

'Joy...?' Marcus looked down at her dazedly as she pulled abruptly away, staring up at him, white-faced. 'What is it?' He frowned at her shocked expression, looking down at her searchingly. 'I'm not trying to rush you.' He shook his head, one hand moving up to caress gently the hotness of her cheek, his frown returning as she flinched away from that touch. 'I want to get to know you first——'

'Before you take me to bed!' She wrenched away from him completely, her eyes flashing deeply green. 'I don't think so, thank you.' She looked at him with contempt. 'You've had a wasted journey, Marcus, because I'm not interested in some sordid little affair with you,' she told him heatedly. 'Maybe you thought I would be a safe bet, because the newspapers aren't likely to pick up on your affair with some unknown woman in a backwater town, but I can assure you it isn't going to happen. I——' She broke off as she heard the sound of a key in the lock of her door.

Casey! His timing, as usual, was awful. But she knew it had to be him; no one else had the key to her flat.

'Joy, I——' Casey looked stunned as he came into the room and saw Marcus there with Joy, although he recovered quickly, looking at the two of them speculatively. 'This is getting to be quite a habit.' He looked questioningly at the other man.

Marcus steadily returned his gaze, his own eyes icy cold. 'I was just about to say the same thing,' he said harshly. 'The two of you live together?' He looked at Joy now. 'Isn't that taking the kissing cousins idea a bit far?'

It was obvious, after the remarks he had made in London too, exactly what Marcus was thinking about the two of them. But it was really none of his business what——

'Hello?' Lisa appeared from behind Casey, almost as tall as he, her gamine features alight with laughter, her flow of golden tresses loose down her back. 'Gosh—Marcus Ballantyne!' Her beautiful face lit up even more, before she thrust out a slender hand towards him. 'Hi, I'm Lisa Goodrich— although, as Casey will tell you, I'm neither good nor rich!' She gave a husky laugh.

Marcus shook her hand briefly, his puzzlement increased, not diminished, by the appearance of this beautiful woman.

'We've just been watching you on television.' Lisa continued to chatter lightly, seeming unaware of the tension that had existed in the room before her sudden appearance—that still existed, as far as Joy was concerned. 'It's very strange to come face to face with you like this straight after that,' Lisa smiled good-naturedly.

It was so exactly how Joy had felt, minutes ago, that she couldn't help sympathising with the lovely Lisa. The two of them had become firm friends during Casey's year-long relationship with the other woman, Joy appreciating Lisa's efforts to stop Casey interfering in her life quite as much as he once had. Although she didn't seem to have been having too much luck at that just lately!

'You're much slimmer than you look on television,' Lisa added, after looking at Marcus appreciatively. 'Just as muscular. And good-looking. But——'

'Yes, I think we all get the general idea, Lisa,' Casey cut in drily. 'Lisa is obviously one of your biggest fans,' he told the other man with a rueful shake of his head.

Marcus glanced towards Joy, dark brows raised. 'It's a pity you can't persuade your lovely cousin here to feel the same way!' he drawled meaningfully.

Heated colour darkened Joy's cheeks. Considering he was here, in her flat, it was a ridiculous thing to say—although she had just been in the process of asking him to leave.

'Gosh, Joy, what are you doing with all this stuff?' Lisa came further into the room, picking up some of the clothes Joy had scattered about. 'You aren't moving, are you?' She frowned. 'Without telling Casey where you're going,' she added teasingly. 'I could quite understand it if you were!' She gave Casey a cheeky grin.

'Lisa never calls me Charles,' Casey told the other man lightly, after shooting Lisa a warning look.

'Why on earth would I call you Charles?' Lisa frowned. 'I—— Oh.' She stopped self-consciously— an unusual occurence for Lisa!—as she realised that, in London, Joy had been Casey. 'We were just on our way out to eat,' she continued, unabashed, 'and wondered if you would like to join us, Joy. You too, of course, Marcus.' She gave him a friendly grin.

'I——'

'We would love to,' Marcus smoothly cut in on Joy's refusal. 'I'm interested to hear about this strange family phenomenon of the name Casey,' he added slowly.

Joy just bet he was! And if the truth was to be told about that, then the truth about the competition would also have to be told—and that was the last thing she wanted. It was bad enough that Marcus believed she had been in London having a fling with an old friend, but to have him know she had been there after Casey won a prize in a competition...! She did have some pride.

She also didn't like the way Marcus had accepted for her the invitation to join Casey and Lisa for a meal. It was arrogant in the extreme. It also meant she had to spend yet more time in Marcus's company.

'I still have a lot to do here.' She indicated the clothes strewn around. 'But the three of you go out for a meal together, by all means,' she invited distantly, sure that Marcus couldn't accept such an invitation on his own; after all, he didn't even know Casey and Lisa.

'Surely this can wait?' Lisa was the one to answer her. 'It can't be that urgent, Joy. And, besides, you have to eat,' she added practically.

Joy would have liked to be able to claim that she had already done so, but she had actually forgotten all about eating once she had started to clear out her wardrobe. Still, a little white lie wouldn't come amiss at a time like this.

'Of course you do,' Marcus said briskly, before she had time to voice her refusal. 'And I'm sure none of us minds waiting the few minutes it's going to take you to change, or tidy your appearance, or whatever other objection you were going to make to the idea.' He looked at her with raised dark brows.

Damn him—he had known exactly what her next remark was going to be! That was because he knew women. He might have been married until five years ago, happily so, as he claimed, but there were sure to have been plenty of other women since that time.

'I'll go and change.' She spoke stiffly, to no one in particular, annoyed with Casey and Lisa for having put her in this position in the first place. Another few minutes and Marcus would have left; now she was being forced to spend yet more time in his company. And that was something she was learning it was dangerous for her to do...

'I'll come with you,' Lisa told her lightly, following her through to the bedroom.

Joy wasn't sure that leaving the two men alone was a good idea. Although she wasn't certain, with Lisa's penchant for bluntness, that leaving her with them would have made the situation any better.

'Wow—he's gorgeous, Joy!' Lisa sat cross-legged on top of Joy's bed while Joy changed into an emerald-green blouse, black waistcoat and matching black trousers—an outfit she had bought earlier that day in an effort to change her image. 'And he obviously feels the same way about you.' Lisa looked at her speculatively as Joy stood in front of the mirror applying her make-up before running a brush through the flaming thickness of her hair. 'That's a great outfit, Joy,' she added admiringly, when Joy made no response to her remarks about Marcus.

'Thank you.' She had to admit that the over-all effect was a good one: smart, but still somehow feminine. But, even so, she felt slightly self-conscious about her appearance. In London, wearing Lisa's clothes, she had been playing a part, but here in her home town she was usually much less noticeable. With Marcus as her escort, that wasn't likely to be the case this evening. She couldn't help wondering what the locals, most of whom she knew, from having lived here all her life and from her job at the library, would think of this celebrity in their midst.

'You look great, Joy.' Casey kissed her lightly on the cheek when they rejoined the two men.

Joy found she couldn't quite look at Marcus—although she could feel the darkness of his gaze on her as he also took in her changed appearance. And she knew he approved. Colour warmed her cheeks yet again as she felt that approval washing over her.

And she felt angry with herself for reacting in that way; what did it matter what Marcus thought of the way she looked? A few minutes ago he had had the nerve to suggest an affair with her. He wanted to get to know her. Wanted her. In every way. He wanted some quiet affair with her—that was more like the truth. And it wasn't going to happen. She wanted her life to change, but not that drastically.

'In view of how lovely the two women look, I suggest we go to the Belmont,' Casey said warmly.

'Is that OK with you, Joy?' Marcus's gaze hadn't left her face, and she knew he must have seen her slight reaction to Casey's suggestion.

The Belmont had been Joy and Gerald's favourite restaurant, although she was sure Casey hadn't thought of that when he suggested it. She and Gerald hadn't gone too often—maybe once a month—because it could be expensive, but nevertheless she had always thought of it as 'their' restaurant. And now she was going there with Marcus...

'Fine.' She still didn't look at him, picking up her jacket and bag. 'Although we should leave now, Casey, or we'll be too late to order.' This wasn't London, where the restaurants seemed to continue serving meals until all hours of the night; nine-thirty was usually the latest time to order a meal in the restaurants here, even the Belmont.

'I'll leave my car here,' Marcus said as they emerged outside and headed for Casey's bright red Escort.

'May as well,' Casey returned good-naturedly, unlocking the car doors for them all.

Joy wasn't too sure about that; it meant Marcus had to come back here to pick his car up. She wasn't sure either about the way he insisted that Lisa sit in the front of the car beside Casey so that he could sit in the back beside her.

Casey and Lisa chattered to Marcus all the way to the restaurant—which was just as well, because Joy couldn't think of a thing to say to him. She would have enjoyed coming out for the evening with Casey and Lisa, but having Marcus along with them was a completely different matter. What did any of them have in common with him? Although Casey and Lisa didn't seem to be having any problems in that direction.

The last thing Joy had expected—or wanted—as she walked into the restaurant at Marcus's side, was to see Gerald sitting at a table near the window—'their' table—with the attractive widow he had dropped Joy for.

How could he? This had been 'their' restaurant, that had been 'their' table—and he was here with that woman! The pain Joy had once felt at Gerald's defection was now replaced by anger, her eyes sparkling with it and a bright flush coming to her cheeks.

Luckily neither Casey or Lisa had noticed the other couple as they were shown to a table across the room from them, and Joy managed to engineer it so that she and Marcus were the ones facing in that direction as they sat down; Casey was not the most tactful of people, and if he had spotted Gerald he would have been sure to say something.

'OK?'

Joy turned to look at Marcus at his gentle query, realising by his searching expression that he had noticed something was wrong. She gave him a bright, meaningless smile. 'Fine,' she lied, inwardly feeling as if she would like to get up, march over to Gerald's table—'their' table—and introduce herself to his companion. It would undoubtedly spoil the other couple's evening for them. But it wouldn't make her feel any better about the situation, was a petty act that would probably make her feel thoroughly miserable, and so she resisted the temptation.

Dark blue eyes still looked at her probingly. 'You seem . . . preoccupied?'

'She's hungry,' Casey put in teasingly. 'If you don't feed Joy on a regular basis, she gets tetchy—to say the least.'

Marcus smiled at the banter. 'I'll remember that,' he said softly.

He wouldn't need to remember it for long; after tonight she never intended seeing him again. 'Let's order, shall we?' she said tautly.

'See what I mean?' Casey grinned across at her. 'She'll be sweet as a pussycat once she's eaten,' he assured the other man confidingly.

Marcus's eyes crinkled at the corners as he looked at her warmly. 'I can hardly wait,' he murmured softly.

He would be waiting a long time before she was 'sweet as a pussycat' to him; it would take more than food to make her like that with him.

'I think your presence is starting to attract some attention,' Lisa remarked lightly to Marcus, when they had all been studying the menu for several minutes.

Lisa was right: people on several of the adjoining tables had realised who Marcus was, glancing his way before talking together in whispers. Marcus continued to look at the menu.

'Doesn't it bother you?' Lisa asked curiously. 'Sometimes people recognise me from my modelling, and I find it very——'

'*That's* where I've seen you before.' Marcus nodded with satisfaction. 'I knew I recognised you from somewhere, Lisa.' He smiled at her.

'Knew the face but couldn't remember the name, hmm?' Joy put in tartly—and instantly regretted it. Not only was it an unecessarily bitchy remark, but she was also being insulting to Lisa. 'Sorry, Lisa,' she muttered uncomfortably. This whole evening was a strain; not only was she having to contend with Marcus, but she also had Gerald and his new woman-friend sitting across the restaurant from her. But that was still no excuse for the remark she had just made.

'No apology for me?' Marcus drawled mockingly.

She looked at him with angry eyes. 'Sorry,' she bit out, the words forced from her lips.

His mouth twisted. 'Very graciously put!'

She was behaving very *un*graciously; she knew she was. But for the moment she was so uptight that she didn't seem to be able to do anything about it. Maybe she would be a little less tense once she had eaten...

'And, no, Lisa, it doesn't bother me,' Marcus lightly answered the other woman, turning to her. 'I work on the premiss that if I ignore them they will soon start to ignore me.'

And, in fact, most people, now they had got over the surprise of recognising the celebrity in their midst, were happily getting on with their meal.

Except the man sitting across the restaurant near the window...

It had only been a matter of time before Gerald became aware of her presence in the restaurant, Joy had known that, and with the attention Marcus was drawing Gerald and his companion were sure to look their way eventually. As Gerald now appeared to have done.

He was openly staring at them, seeming unaware, for the moment, that he was doing so.

'Anyone you know?'

Joy turned sharply to Marcus as he spoke softly against her ear—instantly wishing she hadn't turned quite so suddenly, when she found their faces very close together. But he had spoken softly so that Casey and Lisa, engaged in one of their usual banterings, didn't hear.

She glanced back towards Gerald, only to find that he was still staring at them. Her mouth tightened as she faced Marcus. 'Not any more,' she answered tightly. If she ever had! She had thought she knew Gerald for four years, but the way he had ended their relationship, and his cold behaviour towards her since that time, had given her a different view of him.

Marcus's eyes hardened as he looked across the room at the other man. 'But you did,' he said slowly.

'Yes,' she confirmed tautly, her cheeks flushed at what she knew he must be thinking. For a dowdy librarian, there appeared to be a lot of men in her life. But that was the whole point; appearances could be deceptive. She had gone out with Gerald for four years, no one else, had never been 'out' with Danny Eames, and it had to be obvious by now that Lisa was Casey's girlfriend.

Marcus was looking at her speculatively now, and Joy waited for his next comment apprehensively, especially in front of Casey and Lisa, who were already curious enough about his presence here at all; she had no doubt Casey would give her the third degree once he had her alone.

'Shall we order?' Marcus suggested smoothly as the waiter approached their table.

It was so different from what Joy had been expecting that for a moment she could only stare at him uncomprehendingly. And then she realised he was waiting, dark brows raised questioningly, for her to tell the waiter what she would like to eat.

The four of them gave their orders, and Joy determined not to look in Gerald's direction again. Although she was still furious with him for bringing that woman to 'their' restaurant. The fact that she was here with Casey, Lisa and Marcus wasn't the same thing at all; she was obviously with a party of people, not having a tête-à-tête with another man. Oh, she was aware that there weren't too many restaurants in town, that the choices were limited, but this had been 'their' restaurant...

'So, tell me about the name Casey,' Marcus invited smoothly, once the waiter had poured them each a glass of wine as they waited for the arrival of their food.

Joy shot Casey a warning glance; she still didn't want Marcus to know she had been in London as the prize for a competition. He thought badly enough of her already, but the truth was even more humiliating.

'It's an old family name,' Casey returned, as smoothly, having been schooled by Joy while they were still in London. He shrugged. 'It's just the way some families are.'

'Hmm,' Marcus agreed, unconvinced.

'How's our friend from the taxi?' Casey attempted to change the subject—and instantly chose one that was even more controversial; Danny Eames was already a bone of contention between Joy and Marcus.

Marcus's expression became coolly remote. 'Well, he was nursing a sore head on the set the next day. And a rather sulky expression,' he added dismissively.

'We both know that had nothing to do with the wine he had drunk!' Joy challenged tartly.

Marcus looked at her with cool blue eyes. 'And what did it have to do with?'

There were two bright spots of colour in her cheeks. 'You and I both know——'

'No, I don't think we do,' he interrupted smoothly, although there was a warning glint in the darkness of his eyes. 'And I don't think now is the time to discuss it.' He looked pointedly at Casey and Lisa.

The fact that he was right, and that he had been the one to point out her rudeness, only made Joy even more resentful. They would talk about Danny before Marcus went back to London, and Joy would make her opinion known, once and for all, of Marcus's part in Danny's dismissal. She might find the younger man an idiot and a bore, but that was no reason for Marcus to have taken the action that he obviously had.

'Perhaps not,' she conceded tightly.

'Definitely not,' Marcus bit out, his eyes glacial now.

'But we will,' Joy said stubbornly.

'I'm sure we will.' Marcus nodded abruptly.

They looked challengingly at each other for several seconds, and Joy was the first to look away—an action that irritated her immensely. If they had been on their own...! But they weren't, she accepted impatiently.

'Excuse me.' She stood up abruptly. 'I'm going to the ladies' room,' she explained curtly at Marcus's questioning look.

'The food will be here in a moment,' he reminded her softly.

'I'll be back before then,' she assured him tautly, needing a few minutes to collect herself.

Being out with Marcus was a traumatic enough experience, especially after the things he had said to her earlier at her flat, but her mood certainly wasn't being helped by finding Gerald here at the restaurant with the new woman in his life. Not that she thought a couple of minutes' respite would help to change any of that, but she just had to get away from Marcus's disturbing presence for a few minutes.

Walking straight into Gerald when she emerged from the ladies room five minutes later nullified any effect of calm composure that time on her own might have given her.

CHAPTER EIGHT

'JOY,' he greeted her abruptly.

She couldn't help it; her first instinct was to glance across to where Marcus sat with Casey and Lisa. The three of them were engaged in what appeared to be light-hearted conversation, the two men smiling at something Lisa had just said, none of them looking in Joy's direction.

Thank goodness! After what Marcus had assumed earlier about Gerald and herself, it would probably be better if he didn't see the two of them talking together now. The evening was going to be difficult enough to get through already, without that.

'Gerald.' She returned his greeting as shortly. 'Are you having a good meal?' she added lightly.

'Yes.' He nodded curtly. 'You?'

'We haven't started yet,' Joy dismissed easily. God, this was awful! Why on earth had Gerald decided to speak to her here? Goodness knew they had little enough left to say to each other, without this.

'Your...escort has created quite a lot of attention.' Gerald glanced across at Marcus with hard eyes.

Just at that moment, as if sensing the interest, Marcus looked across at the two of them, his expression tightening momentarily before a bland façade took its place.

'That is Marcus Ballantyne, isn't it?' Gerald frowned.

None other. And Joy was finding she couldn't look away from the intensity of those dark blue eyes. Marcus didn't show by so much as a movement of a muscle that he was angry at seeing Gerald talking to her in this way, and yet Joy knew that he was—very angry.

But he didn't have the right to be! He might have declared his intentions towards her earlier, might want her, to have an affair with her, but those were his feelings towards her, not hers for him.

What were her feelings towards Marcus? She had tried, during the time since her return from London, not to look too deeply into her uncharacteristic response to Marcus, but now that he had turned up here...

If Casey and Lisa hadn't arrived at her flat at the time they had, would she really have had the strength, the emotional strength, to say no to Marcus? Emotional strength? What...?

Joy felt all the colour drain from her face as the truth hit her, a truth she wanted to deny—desperately—but couldn't. She was in love with Marcus.

'Joy?' Gerald was looking at her concernedly now as he too saw the change in her expression.

She was in love with Marcus!

She looked at Gerald, saw only a stranger, someone she had thought she knew, but obviously hadn't. Someone she had thought she loved, but, in comparison with the emotions that had now hit her concerning Marcus, she knew she had never loved Gerald either. Not like this. Not with this all-consuming need.

Oh, God, no, she couldn't feel this way about Marcus. He was a man completely out of her sphere, a man who had lived a life she could know nothing about, a life she would have no hope of fitting into.

Not even as his mistress.

She couldn't be that to him, either. It would belittle what she felt for him to have that sort of fleeting relationship with him. But not to be in his life at all...

She wished he had never come here, with his presence forcing her to acknowledge the feelings she had been so strongly denying to herself. Oh, she had reasoned, defensively used logic to explain her reaction to him. And all the time she had been in love with him.

'Joy, I need to talk to you——'

'Not now, Gerald,' she cut in distractedly, wondering how on earth she was going to return to the table with the knowledge she now had of her feelings towards Marcus; it was going to be impossible.

'But, Joy——'

'Not now, Gerald.' She held up her hand impatiently, too disturbed now even to look in Marcus's direction to see if he was still watching them.

'I'll call you tomorrow, shall I?' Gerald suggested anxiously. 'We really do need to talk, Joy. We——'

'I thought we were leaving, Gerald?' His companion of the evening had suddenly appeared at his side, apparently from the cloakroom, wearing a jacket over her dress now, her handbag slung over

her shoulder. 'Aren't you going to introduce us?'
Hard blue eyes looked pointedly at Joy.

Gerald looked totally disconcerted now, a slightly
hunted look on his face. 'Doreen, this is one of the
young ladies from the library, Joy Simms. Joy,
my...friend, Doreen Lane,' he finally introduced
awkwardly.

Joy knew from the sudden narrowing of those
blue eyes that Doreen knew exactly who this 'young
lady from the library' was. The other woman shook
her hand briefly—very briefly—her smile not
reaching her eyes.

Not that Joy could exactly blame her; this was
a very difficult meeting for all of them. It was surprising it had never happened before, although
Joy's preferred lack of a social life during the last
six months had probably aided that. And, considering the circumstances in which it had happened, it couldn't have come at a worse time for
Joy.

Or perhaps it was the best time? She certainly
wasn't feeling any pain from this meeting, was too
caught up in her realised emotions towards Marcus.
Maybe, after all, it was the best time for this to
have happened...

'Nice to have met you,' she told the other woman
brightly, her own smile at least as genuine as the
other woman's. 'Enjoy the rest of your evening,'
she told them in parting, sure, from her knowledge
of Gerald, that this was actually the end of their
evening; Gerald liked to be home and in his bed by
ten-thirty at night, claiming that he needed at least
eight hours' sleep a night.

She didn't give Gerald—or Doreen—a chance to say anything further, walking determinedly across the restaurant to rejoin Marcus, Lisa and Casey. Not that she particularly wanted to be there either; she would rather have been at home right now, nursing her invaded heart, but she couldn't leave when they hadn't even eaten yet.

'How was your old friend?' Marcus drawled lightly as she sat down next to him.

She knew he had seen her talking to Gerald—his disapproval had been obvious even across the restaurant. She should have known he would refer to the incident. Marcus could never be accused of holding back when he had something to say—and he wasn't about to let the incident he had witnessed across the room pass without comment.

'What old friend?' Casey looked puzzled, still completely unaware of Gerald's presence in the restaurant.

Gerald and Doreen had left now—thank goodness! 'Just someone I work with,' Joy dismissed easily, giving Casey a warning look as his eyes widened knowingly before he glanced round. 'He's gone now,' she added drily, as Casey turned back to her questioningly.

'Was he alone?' Casey asked with feigned innocence, dark brows raised mockingly in Joy's direction.

'He appeared to have his wife with him,' Marcus put in coolly.

'Oh, he——'

'Are you all waiting for me?' Joy cut in lightly seeing that their starters had arrived in her absence.

'Let's eat before the food gets cold.' And drop the subject of Gerald and his companion.

Marcus obviously still thought Gerald was an ex-lover of hers, a married ex-lover, and she really felt too weary at this moment to try and explain herself to him. Besides, why should she? Marcus wanted to be her lover himself, so he had no right to judge any of her past relationships with anyone else.

It was difficult for her to eat the food she had ordered, her appetite—what little she had had to start with—having completely deserted her. She loved Marcus Ballantyne. Could it be called love when she hardly knew him? Or was it just an intense sexual attraction? How could she know any more?

She had thought she loved Gerald, but seeing him tonight had shown her otherwise. She had felt nothing towards him personally, or at seeing him with Doreen. She hadn't liked the fact that he had brought the other woman here, but that had only been an initial resentment at seeing him in 'their' restaurant with someone else. It had nothing to do with jealousy of the other woman, which she would surely have felt if there were even the remnants left of any feelings she had once had towards Gerald.

Besides, she had never felt the excitement in Gerald's company that she felt whenever she was with Marcus...

But was that love either? She didn't know any more, felt thoroughly confused.

'You've gone very quiet.' Marcus spoke softly at her side, when their plates had been removed.

In truth, the conversation between the other three people at the table had passed completely over her head for the last ten minutes or so, so lost in thought had she been. But she looked at Marcus now, sure that some of her confusion must be evident in her expression, but at a loss to do anything about it. She was confused. Completely. She had never realised that loving someone involved feeling a warm glow from just looking at the person you felt the emotion for. As she did looking at Marcus now.

She *did* love him!

Now, what was she going to do about it? He had offered her an affair, obviously felt enough attraction towards her to have sought her out to offer her at least that. But was it enough? Joy had a feeling that was something she was going to have to decide before they left the restaurant to go home this evening . . .

'Where are you staying tonight?'

Casey's question came as they all sat in Joy's apartment drinking coffee, the evening not having been quite the disaster Joy had thought it might be. Casey and Lisa had been in good form, their banter filling in any awkward moments there might have been.

However, Casey's question now seemed to have caused one, complete silence following the casual query, with Joy staring down into her coffee-cup; she had been wondering the same thing for most of the evening.

'I don't think that's any of our business, Casey,' Lisa softly rebuked, shaking her head at his lack of tact.

Casey frowned. 'I only asked because it's a bit late to be booking in anywhere locally, and I thought Marcus might like to crash out at my flat——' Casey broke off with a pained wince as he finally realised why Lisa thought it was none of their business where Marcus stayed tonight. 'Perhaps not,' he grimaced, looking uncomfortable now.

'I appreciate the offer, Casey,' Marcus told him smoothly.

But he hadn't refused or accepted it, Joy realised. What was that supposed to mean? He couldn't stay here. Could he...?

Lisa gave a pointed yawn. 'I'm ready to go now, Case, if you are?'

'Sure,' he agreed, obviously deciding he had been tactless enough for one evening. 'Nice to have met you again, Marcus.' He shook the other man's hand warmly.

'We'll meet again,' Marcus assured him smilingly.

'I hope we do!' Lisa was much more forthcoming, reaching up to kiss Marcus on the cheek.

Joy said her own goodnights as if in a daze, wondering what she was going to do once Lisa and Casey had gone. Marcus had made it plain what he wanted. But was it what she wanted too?

'I thought I told you not to call me Case,' Casey was complaining to Lisa as they let themselves out.

'Oh, stop being such an old grump,' Lisa retaliated good-naturedly.

Casey was still muttering as they disappeared outside, slamming the door behind them.

'They're always like that,' Joy told Marcus awkwardly, shooting him a nervous glance. 'They don't mean anything by it.'

She felt very self-conscious now that the two of them were alone. She wasn't sure what was going to happen next.

'Who was the man, Joy?' Marcus watched her from across the room with narrowed eyes.

She was so taken aback by the question that for a moment she could only stare back at him; it was so far removed from what she had thought he was going to say. Although quite what that was she didn't know either. But certainly not this.

'I said earlier.' She shrugged dismissively. 'Someone I work with at the library. You didn't know I was a librarian, did you?' she added challengingly.

'You might be surprised at what I know, Joy,' Marcus drawled drily.

She stiffened defensively. 'Such as what?'

He shrugged. 'You're twenty-seven years old. You've worked at the local library for the last five years. Your parents live in——'

'You didn't get all that from the people at the hotel?' Joy gasped indignantly.

'Just your name and address,' he agreed. 'Casey supplied the rest while you were in your room changing earlier.'

Damn Casey! She should have known he couldn't be trusted to be alone with Marcus.

'I think he wanted to tell me about the birthmark on your left shoulder too,' Marcus added, at her obvious outrage at what she considered her cousin's betrayal. 'But I already know about that,' he said softly, getting slowly to his feet.

Colour entered her cheeks as she remembered the circumstances in which he had come to know about that. 'It's getting late, Marcus. And I——' She broke off. No, she didn't have to work in the morning, it was Saturday—her day off. 'It's getting late,' she said again firmly.

'And you want me to leave,' he offered.

Wasn't that obvious? 'I think it might be best.' She nodded.

'I've told you I'm not going to rush this, Joy——'

'There's nothing to rush, Marcus,' she cut in firmly. 'It's been nice seeing you——'

'But now go away again?' he drawled.

'Yes.' She faced him determinedly, although inside she was quaking.

She loved this man, a man way, way out of her sphere, a man whose face was known worldwide, as was his talent. Who would have believed one trip to London would have such a life-changing effect? For her. Because she would never be the same, having loved this man. And it had to become loved. In the past. As quickly as possible.

'I don't want this, Marcus,' she told him firmly.

'This?' He arched dark brows.

Joy shook her head. 'Any of this,' she said agitatedly. 'You're an intelligent man, Marcus, you have to understand what I mean.'

He looked at her steadily for several seconds, holding her gaze. Joy forced herself to hold that look. If she once wavered...

'All right, Joy,' he said at last heavily. 'You win. I'll go.' He picked up the jacket he had removed earlier, shrugging his broad shoulders into it.

It wasn't a question of winning, it was a question of survival for her. This way, never having made love with Marcus, she at least stood a chance of getting over her feelings for him. But if she was in his arms even once more...

'But I'm in the area for several more days,' he told her abruptly. 'If you should change your mind about seeing me, I'm at this hotel.' He took a card from the breast-pocket of his jacket and put it down on the coffee-table. 'I booked in there earlier today,' he explained, at her questioning look.

He had had somewhere to stay tonight all the time! The knowledge only sharpened her resolve for him to leave. If she had invited him to stay, he would never have told her about the hotel booking. No wonder he hadn't taken up Casey's offer of staying with him!

'You had better go,' she told him tautly, her eyes flashing deeply green. Maybe the sort of game he had been playing all evening was acceptable in the circles he mixed in in London, but it certainly wasn't acceptable to her. 'Now!' she added angrily.

She was angry with herself, more than anything. She had believed Marcus was different, had wanted to believe he was different, and he had just proved himself as capable of duplicity as any other man.

'Joy!' Suddenly he was close to her, very close, his arms moving strongly about her waist to pull her up against him, his body hard and unyielding.

It was the one thing she had hoped he wouldn't do; her strength was only a very thin veneer. And when he held her in his arms like this, it wasn't even a veneer.

'Look at me, Joy,' Marcus instructed softly.

She didn't want to do that. Because if she did, she didn't know if she would be able to keep to her resolve to ask him to go.

'Joy...'

She couldn't resist looking up at him. It was too much to ask of herself not to. And, as she did so, she melted under the fierce tenderness of those deep blue eyes, uanble to look away, held captive.

His kiss, when it came, was soft and gentle, his mouth moving searchingly against hers. And it was more potent than if he had demanded a response from her; Joy returned the kisses with a gentle passion of her own.

At last Marcus raised his head, his hands moving up to cradle her face. 'I want to get to know you, Joy. And I want you to get to know me,' he added huskily. 'Let me take you out to lunch tomorrow?'

She wasn't working; it was her day off. But did she want to get to know this man? Wasn't that a dangerous thing to do? Dangerous or not, how could she resist?

'Marcus, I'm not——' His fingertips were placed softly over her lips, stopping her words. Joy looked up at him with wide green eyes.

'Who knows what you're not—or, indeed, what I'm not,' he added self-derisively, 'until we get to know each other? Isn't it enough, for the moment, that we do want to learn more about each other?'

It was more than she had thought he wanted, and yet, even so...

'Lunch tomorrow,' he said again decisively. 'And if you decide you don't want to see me again after that, well... Then I'll have to accept that, won't I?' Although he didn't look too happy about the idea. 'What do you have to lose, Joy?' he added teasingly.

So much more than he could possibly realise! But lunch—surely that was harmless enough?

She gazed up at him for several more long, tense moments, and then she gave an inward sigh of defeat; she wanted to have lunch with him. 'Lunch,' she nodded. 'But that's——' Again his fingertips on her lips stopped further speech.

'I'll call for you at twelve-thirty. Is that all right?' he prompted softly, removing his fingertips so that she could answer him.

Joy couldn't help the smile that curved her lips and added a glow to the green of her eyes. 'You aren't used to asking for what you want, are you?' she mocked lightly.

He gave a self-derisive laugh. 'Is it that obvious?'

'Yes!' Joy laughed too now.

Marcus shook his head. 'Would it be very arrogant on my part to say I don't usually have to ask?' He tilted his head, his expression quizzical.

'Incredibly arrogant!' But she couldn't help laughing again, relieved at the release of tension that had existed between them all evening.

'You're beautiful when you laugh,' he told her huskily, the laughter rapidly fading as his eyes darkened with passion.

Joy saw that passion—and already knew how dangerous it was. They were alone in her flat, the sexual tension between them was high—she acknowledged now that it always had been—and it would be too easy for them just to go to bed right now and make love. And then what? Joy inwardly shook at the devastation that would leave in her life.

'You have to go, Marcus,' she told him as she moved out of his arms. 'I had a lovely evening,' she added politely.

'But now it has to end,' he realised pointedly.

'Yes,' she agreed firmly. 'Thank you for dinner.' To her acute embarrassment, and she was sure to Lisa's and Casey's too, Marcus had insisted on paying for dinner for them all. No amount of argument on their part would budge him. That arrogance again, no doubt. 'Lunch tomorrow is on me,' she added challengingly.

'I invited you,' he reminded her mockingly.

'And I accept, on condition that I pay,' Joy told him calmly, having no intention of letting him pay for lunch too.

Marcus's mouth quirked as he looked down at her. 'You're a woman of conditions, are you?' he taunted softly.

'Not that I'm aware of.' She shook her head, meeting his gaze unflinchingly.

'All right, lunch is on you,' he nodded. 'But don't think I'll give in this easily on everything,' he added warningly.

Joy hadn't made any assumptions whatsoever where this man was concerned, and she had a feeling she never would. Never? That made it sound as if she would continue to see him after they had lunch tomorrow—even though she had already decided earlier it wouldn't be a good idea to see him again at all. Her resolve where this man was concerned seemed to be nil!

'Twelve-thirty tomorrow,' Marcus put in quickly, seeming to sense her sudden inward panic. 'By the way, I like your cousin,' he added as he walked to the door. 'Now all we have to sort out is the role of Danny Eames in your life, and the man in the restaurant this evening. I'm sure there's a reasonable explanation for both of them.' There had better be, his tone implied.

Joy gave an indignant gasp but, before she could manage to find a cutting reply, Marcus had given her a brief kiss on the lips before letting himself out of the door and closing it quietly behind him. Of all the arrogant——! But he *was* arrogant, Joy accepted almost limply; he acknowledged it himself. Who else but a man of extreme arrogance would have gone to the trouble to search her out in her home in the first place?

And she was committed to having lunch with him tomorrow.

What else had she committed herself to by accepting his invitation? *Her* invitation, because she was the one who had insisted on paying—literally—for the privilege of putting herself in this state of complete confusion!

Quarter past twelve!

Marcus had said more than once that he would call for her at twelve-thirty. And yet he was ringing her doorbell, and it was only twelve-fifteen.

And Joy wasn't even halfway ready; she had been in the shower until a few minutes ago, had dressed in a short black skirt and deep green silk overblouse, but hadn't yet had time to apply her makeup or dry her hair. Her hair, she realised now, was going to be a lost cause, but there was no way she was going to open the door to Marcus with her face completely bare of make-up; he had already seen her in too many states of disarray during their brief—very brief—acquaintance. He would just have to wait while she applied foundation, blusher, and some lipstick.

While she quickly carried out this task the doorbell rang twice more, irritating her immensely; her cheeks were barely in need of any blusher in her agitation.

Her hair, meanwhile, had dried in bright red curls down her back; she usually straightened those curls out while drying her hair, as she didn't particularly like the slightly gypsy-like appearance this more unruly style gave her. Oh, well, she was changing her style, including her hair, with a vengeance.

Her eyes sparkled, and her cheeks glowed quite naturally when she finally marched over to wrench open the door to her flat.

Her mouth almost fell open in surprise as she saw her visitor.

Gerald!

CHAPTER NINE

WHAT on earth was he doing here?

He couldn't be here! Marcus would be here at any minute; at least five minutes had elapsed since Gerald had first begun to ring her doorbell. The last thing she needed, or wanted, was for Marcus to find her with yet another man. Especially after the assumptions she knew he had made last night, where Gerald was concerned. And, because she had been so annoyed, she had let him go on assuming.

Of course—twelve-fifteen; Gerald always took his lunch-hour between twelve and one o'clock. He must have driven straight from the library to see her here. He was certainly dressed as he would normally be for work, in a tailored dark suit and white shirt, accompanied by a conservatively patterned tie in nondescript colours.

She knew he had said they had to talk, but he had said he would call her, not come here to see her in person. And he was the last person she wanted to see just now.

'I know it's your day off——'

'I'm going out, Gerald,' she told him abruptly, making no move to open the door to allow him inside.

He seemed to take in her appearance for the first time, brown eyes widening with speculation at her loose hair and the short length of her skirt. 'So I see,' he said slowly. 'The thing is, Joy, I really need to talk to you. Last night——'

'Our meal was wonderful too,' she cut in brightly, all the time she was talking to him shooting anxious looks behind him in case Marcus should arrive at the top of the stairs.

Gerald looked irritated. 'I didn't want to talk about the meal, Joy,' he dismissed impatiently. 'Doreen and I had an argument after leaving the restaurant.'

'I'm sorry.' She frowned. And she was, genuinely sorry. She hadn't particularly taken to the other woman, but Gerald had seemed to like her, and it was a pity if they were now at odds with each other. Although she didn't see what business it was of hers...

'The argument was to do with you, actually,' Gerald continued. 'Look, Joy, couldn't I come inside? We can talk more privately in there.'

She didn't want to talk to him more privately, had nothing to say to him. She was sorry if her presence in the restaurant last night had caused some strain between Gerald and Doreen, but really that was for the other couple to sort out between themselves. Besides, it must be twelve-thirty by now, and at any moment Marcus was going to walk up the stairs and see her standing here talking to Gerald—a man he had assumed was married—a man she had let him assume she had had an affair with.

She shook her head. 'I really do have to go now, Gerald,' she told him almost breathlessly.

He didn't look at all pleased by her offhand attitude. 'Well, if you insist,' he said stiffly. 'Perhaps I could call in this evening?'

That wasn't a good idea either; she had no idea when she would be back from her lunch with Marcus, or if, indeed, she would be alone when she did return. And a face-to-face meeting between these two men was something she was trying to avoid at all costs.

'I'll telephone you later today and we can sort out a time for us to meet,' she said—and it wouldn't necessarily be here. She had no idea why Gerald was suddenly being so persistent about talking to her; she had told him repeatedly during the last week that she had no intention of changing her mind about staying on at the library. And they had nothing else to talk about. 'And a place,' she added firmly.

His face took on a pained look. 'Joy, I know I wasn't very kind to you last year——'

'Not now, Gerald.' She was becoming panicked now, and that panic was starting to show in her voice. She just wanted him to go away. Enough wrong assumptions had already been made between herself and Marcus; she didn't want there to be any more because of Gerald's presence at her flat. 'I said I'll call you.'

He gave a heavy sigh. 'I suppose your coldness is the least I can expect after the way I behaved towards you.'

She wasn't cold—she was completely uninterested, in Gerald, and anything he might have to say.

'I only hope——' he reached out to clasp one of her hands in both of his '—that in time you'll be able to forgive me.'

'You're forgiven, Gerald,' she told him impatiently, pulling her hand away; that was the last thing she wanted Marcus to see—Gerald being here at all was bad enough.

His face brightened, a smile in his eyes. 'So you think there's still hope for us?'

Hope for them? She frowned. What on earth did he mean now?

'There's nothing serious between you and—and Marcus Ballantyne?' Gerald looked unsure of himself.

There would be nothing at all between Marcus and herself if she didn't get rid of Gerald—now!

'Of course not,' she snapped dismissively, glancing at her watch. Twelve twenty-nine. And Marcus was nothing if not punctual. 'I'll call you later, Gerald,' she said again, almost desperately.

'It's more than I could have hoped for.' Once again he reached out and clasped her hand, briefly this time. 'I'll look forward to your call.'

Joy closed the door behind him with such relief that her knees felt weak. And she promptly put Gerald from her mind. After six months of wondering where she had gone wrong with him, she no longer cared. Something the last couple of weeks had shown her was that Gerald had always been wrong for her. Married to him, she would have been old before her time, her life as narrow as Gerald's own was, living within the confines of what was expected of her. Now she was free, totally free, to make her own decisions, live her own life, in the way that she decided to live it.

But did that include becoming Marcus's mistress? That was still something she didn't know. She knew only that she wanted to see him again, that she had been in a state of high expectation all morning as she looked forward to this lunch with him. And——

This time when the doorbell rang she knew it had to be Marcus. Exactly on time, at twelve-thirty. Thank God she had got rid of Gerald before he arrived!

Her breath caught in her throat as she looked up at Marcus, her pulse racing at how attractive he looked in black fitted trousers, a pale grey shirt and a charcoal-grey jacket, the darkness of his hair looking still slightly damp from a shower. But it was his eyes, those fascinating blue eyes, that held her captive and took her breath away as he darkly returned her gaze.

'I'm not too early, am I?' he said huskily.

No—thank God! A few minutes earlier than this and he would have been. 'Of course not.' She smiled brightly, opening the door wider for him to come inside. 'Would you like a drink, or something, before we leave?' she offered, once she had closed the door behind him.

He turned to her, a sardonic smile curving his lips. 'Now, there's a leading question,' he murmured softly, his gaze sweeping approvingly over her own appearance.

'I meant coffee. Or wine,' Joy said drily.

'I'll give the coffee a miss. The wine too. Unless you already have some open?' He raised dark brows.

Joy gave him a sharp look. Just what was he implying now? That she was a secret wino?

Calm down, Joy, she inwardly instructed herself; she was far too tense and hypersensitive where this man was concerned, over-reacting to almost everything he had to say.

'No, I don't.' She forced herself to smile naturally. 'But I don't mind opening a bottle, if you would like some.'

He shrugged. 'Only if you would like some yourself.'

They were talking together like polite strangers now. But maybe that would be best for a while; the whole atmosphere had been far too charged between them since the moment they had first met.

She glanced at her wristwatch. 'I've actually booked a table at a local restaurant for twelve-forty-five, so we could have a drink once we get there, if you would like one.'

'Fine.' Marcus nodded abruptly. 'Do you have a coat? It's quite cold out there.'

She still had the bright red Cossack-style coat that Lisa had lent her for her trip to London. She went into her bedroom to collect it, shivering slightly with anticipation as Marcus took the coat from her and held it out for her to slip her arms in.

'You have beautiful hair,' he told her gruffly as he moved around in front of her to reach up and put his hands beneath its long silky length and release it from the confines of the coat collar.

It was such an intimate gesture, one of his hands now lightly caressing a long wayward curl, that Joy could feel the heated colour in her cheeks. He was standing so close to her now that she could see the slightly darker flecks in the clear blue of his eyes, the slight shadow of a beard on his chin—that square, aggressive chin with its arrogantly set jawline.

Her breathing was slightly uneven, all her senses heightened, her hands shaking slightly as she thrust them into her coat pockets. And this was before they even went out for lunch; she was going to be a gibbering wreck after spending a few hours in his company!

'We'll be late for the restaurant,' she finally had to remark—if they didn't leave soon, she had a feeling they wouldn't do so at all.

'Are you hungry?'

Joy looked up at him sharply, swallowing hard as she saw the warm caress in his eyes, knowing by that warmth that she hadn't imagined the double edge to Marcus's remark. God, yes, she was hungry—hungry to know his kisses once again, the feel of his hands on her body, the hardness of his own need . . .

She swayed weakly towards him, drawn to that warmth emanating from his body; the touch of his hands, as they rested on her shoulders after releasing her hair, seemed to burn through the thickness of her coat.

'Because I am,' he added, before abruptly moving away from her. 'I had an appointment early this morning and woke up too late to have breakfast, so I'm starving now.'

Joy was still slightly dazed from the sexual tension that had seemed to burn between them so intensely—before it had been so abruptly broken by Marcus.

'Shall we go?' He waited expectantly for her by the door.

She was sure she hadn't imagined that warmth in his eyes, or the caress of his hands against her shoulders, and yet to look at him now, they might never have been. He looked distant, remote even, the enquiry on the hardness of his face as he waited to leave that of a polite stranger.

And they were far from being strangers; they were on the point of becoming lovers. Joy was convinced of it. And she trembled at the thought.

Once they were in Marcus's car their time was taken up by Joy giving Marcus directions to the restaurant. She had chosen a hotel just out of town for their lunch. She had been there several times in the past in the evening for a drink with Gerald, but had never actually eaten in the restaurant itself, although she knew it had a good reputation. It had been difficult to think of somewhere suitable to take Marcus; she only hoped the food was as good as it was reputed to be.

It was a typical country hotel; a grand old manor-house, with ivy growing over the grey brick walls, genuine antique furniture inside the building adding to its old-worlde charm, and huge vases of flowers making splashes of colour among the faded elegance.

'Very nice.' Marcus nodded, a properitorial hand under Joy's elbow as they entered the reception area.

She felt a warm glow at his approval; she had wanted to choose somewhere he would like.

'Good-evening—I mean, good afternoon, Miss Simms,' the receptionist greeted her warmly. The young girl was an avid reader, a regular in the library on her days off from working in the hotel. 'Sorry.' Jennifer gave an embarrassed laugh. 'I'm not used to seeing you here during the day,' she explained to Joy awkwardly, her eyes widening as she obviously recognised Joy's escort.

Marcus looked down at Joy, his brows raised. 'And just when *is* she used to seeing you at the hotel?' he murmured, so that only Joy could hear him.

Joy frowned. 'I——'

'You have a table booked for lunch in the restaurant, I believe,' Jennifer continued brightly, although her astounded gaze was still fixed on Marcus.

That reaction from strangers again, Joy realised a little uncomfortably, although Marcus was doing his usual trick of ignoring the recognition. She supposed that after all these years it was easy to do, although Joy wasn't sure she would ever have got used to it.

'Yes,' Joy answered the young girl lightly.

'If you would just like to go through, someone will take your coat and give you the menus,' Jennifer told them. 'Enjoy your meal, Miss Simms. Mr Ballantyne,' she added a little breathlessly.

Marcus gave her one of those slightly wolfish, heart-stopping smiles of his that had lit up film and television screens for years, although he seemed to forget the very existence of the young girl as they strolled through to the restaurant.

'Don't worry about it so much,' Marcus murmured at Joy's side as they entered the restaurant and he helped her off with her coat. 'She gave me something by recognising me in the first place; I gave her something back by acknowledging that.' He shrugged dismissively. 'Everybody gets something from the encounter.'

Joy had never quite looked at it in that way before. Marcus had probably made Jennifer's day by smiling at her in the way that he had, and it must obviously be pleasing to be talented enough to be instantly known in the way that Marcus was. That constant recognition didn't seem quite so awe-inspiring when looked at in that light.

They were shown straight to their table, and this time Joy was able to ignore the situation when Marcus was recognised by staff and lunchers alike.

'Have you been here often?' Marcus looked about him appreciatively. Their table faced out into the garden which sloped down to a lake about a quarter of a mile away.

'A few times,' she confirmed. 'Did you go anywhere interesting this morning?' God, they were being polite, weren't they? 'You said you missed breakfast because you had an early appointment.' And maybe, just maybe, she shouldn't have asked him that; it was, after all, rather a personal question.

'It wasn't actually that early,' he drawled dismissively. 'I just overslept because I couldn't get to sleep last night.' And the broodingly dark look he gave her told her exactly why he had had trouble sleeping the night before.

Joy looked away from that compellingly dark gaze. She had had the same problem herself; she had lain awake for hours after Marcus had left, burning with an ache only he could assuage.

'Your town has a small theatre.' He spoke softly, but his seemingly sudden change of subject caused Joy to look across the table at him frowningly. 'I have a play I want to run in the provinces before taking it to the West End. I spoke with the manager of the threatre this morning about a week's run here in the autumn.'

He wasn't changing the subject at all; he was answering her question. '*You* spoke with the manager?' Joy frowned. 'Isn't it rather unusual for the star of the play to do that sort of thing?' She couldn't believe an actor of his stature had to organise his own theatre runs.

He gave a crooked smile. 'I didn't say I was the star of the play,' he mused. 'Actually——' He broke off as the waiter came to take their order for drinks. 'Joy?'

She distractedly gave her request for a glass of white wine, too interested in what Marcus was saying to welcome the interruption. He might be coming back to the area in the autumn...

'You were saying?' she prompted, as soon as they were alone again.

'I run a production company, Joy,' he explained lightly. 'Nothing too big, we only do one or two productions a year, but it adds a certain spice to my career, gives me a day job, so to speak,' he added wryly. 'My company is actually involved in the production of *Pilgrim's Game*,' he added softly.

And at last Joy had her answer to how Marcus had so much influence in the decisions made concerning the programme, such as Danny's dismissal. Marcus hadn't needed to throw his weight around at all; he just made a production decision, and it was carried out. It explained exactly how it had been done so easily, but it still didn't excuse the fact that it had been done at all.

'Shall we order our food?' Joy suggested stiffly, when the waiter returned with their drinks and stood poised to take their order.

There was a stilted silence once the waiter had again departed—at least, to Joy it felt stilted. She had tried not to think too much about Danny, and Marcus's part in his dismissal, but now it had been brought back into sharp focus once again. Everything she had learnt about Marcus pointed to his being a man determined to have his own way; she just hadn't liked to think about him having gone as far as he had where Danny was concerned.

Because she was in love with Marcus. But, then, who liked to think of the person they loved as having done something they themselves considered unfair and unwarranted? It didn't change the emotions she felt towards Marcus, it just——

'You've gone very quiet,' he pointedly cut in on her troubled thoughts.

She forced a bright smile to her lips. 'Have I?'

He nodded. 'You know you have. And don't smile if it isn't what you want to do,' he added harshly. 'Be yourself, Joy; that's what I like about you. And, looking at you, I would say smiling at me is the last thing on your mind.'

She stared across the table at him. Why was it that this man was so astute when it came to her emotions? Surely it had to be more than just body language, as he called it. Because he seemed to know what she was feeling a lot of the time before she even knew it herself.

As long as he didn't realise she loved him. That would be just too humiliating. An offered affair was one thing; love was something else.

'It's about Danny,' she began hesitantly, loath to bring a note of discord to the day, but knowing she couldn't keep silent on the subject now that it was so much on her mind.

Marcus sighed. 'Surely you've realised by now that Danny is his own worst enemy? He breaks contractual agreements, is unreliable, has—— God, I didn't come all this way to talk about Danny Eames!' Marcus snapped impatiently. 'Far too much of my time lately has been given over to thinking about that particular young man—and, quite frankly, he isn't worth it.' Blue eyes glittered angrily.

Joy could see that he felt very strongly about Danny and his behaviour, and maybe, just maybe, she didn't really know enough about the situation to judge...

'I would actually,' Marcus continued softly, his gaze intent, 'much rather we talked about the man who left your flat earlier. If we have to talk about another man at all,' he added grimly.

He had seen Gerald leave her flat! She wasn't even sure herself what he had been doing there. All she had been able to think about at the time was that Marcus would be arriving at any moment and Gerald had to be gone before he did. It hadn't even occurred to her that the two men's paths might have crossed once Gerald was outside.

'Gerald is a colleague,' she said stiltedly.

'You said last night that he was someone you used to know.' Marcus held her captive with that dark gaze. 'Why would an old friend be calling round at your flat today?'

'Marcus——'

'Joy!' he returned harshly, his mouth a thin, grim line now.

She had sensed a tension about him from the moment he had arrived earlier, and this was obviously the reason for it. But Gerald was a humiliating part of her life, one she was trying to forget. She didn't particularly want to talk about him, or the pain he had inflicted on her last year by his defection.

'I was ... involved with him. But I'm not now,' she added firmly. 'And I don't want to talk about him.' She met Marcus's gaze challengingly now.

'We'll have to talk about him some time,' he said softly.

Her eyes widened. 'Why will we?'

'Because he's still there, Joy,' Marcus pointed out.

'And are you going to give me a detailed account of all the people in your life, past and present?' she returned defensively, completely unconcerned with the waiter bringing the food to their table, two bright spots of indignant colour in her cheeks.

He shrugged, for the moment also ignoring the food that had been placed in front of them. 'The past, you know about. I was married, my wife died. There have been perhaps two or three relationships since then, but nothing serious. Now, I know you aren't the bored wife out for a week of fun in London that I assumed you were when we first met, but at the same time I realise a beautiful woman like you must have had men in your life. And the man from this morning appears to have been one of them,' he added grimly.

Gerald had been the only man in her life to date, and even then it hadn't been in the way she was sure Marcus meant. And she wasn't at all flattered at being called beautiful, because she knew that she wasn't. 'I really don't think talking about the past is of any relevance to anything,' she dismissed firmly, picking up her spoon to drink her soup. 'It usually just adds to the confusion.'

'The man from this morning——'

'His name is Gerald,' she cut in tautly.

'OK—Gerald.' Marcus shrugged. 'He isn't in the past.'

As far as she was concerned, he was. Completely in the past.

'He seems to be slightly older than you,' Marcus persisted as he started his own soup. 'A classic case of a young woman falling for the married father figure?'

Joy was uncomfortable with this whole conversation. Yes, Gerald was 'slightly older' than she was, but it had been something she hadn't really been aware of until recently. 'Gerald isn't married,' she snapped defensively.

A strange expression flickered across Marcus's face, so fleeting that it was difficult to tell what it had meant. 'I see,' he finally said slowly. 'How is your soup?'

She didn't know; she hadn't tasted any of it. She had been eating automatically, disturbed by the subject of the conversation. 'Fine,' she answered abruptly.

'Joy——' Marcus reached out and clasped her hand with his '—I don't mean to pry——'

'Then don't!' she snapped again. 'Tell me more about the play you're intending to tour with. You aren't starring in it, you said?'

For a moment it looked as if he wouldn't accept this change of subject, and then he gave a slight shrug before answering her question. 'I'm directing, not acting.' He went on to talk about his first attempt at directing, the buzz of excitement he was getting from it. 'Acting on its own is beginning to pall,' he finished with a grimace. 'Oh, I don't intend to stop.' He smiled ruefully at her surprised expression. 'Just change course for a short while.'

A bit like Joy, with her decision to change the staleness of her own life. How strange that they should both have decided on this change at the same time. And she had thought they had nothing in common!

It was a lunch without controversy, now that they had closed the subject of Joy's personal life, and, as the meal progressed and the wine flowed, Joy began to relax completely, enjoying Marcus's sense of humour—sharp and even wicked at times—as he told her some of the anecdotes from his years of acting.

'A lot of that is not really for public knowledge,' he mused, as he lightly held her elbow as they left the restaurant two hours later. 'It would shatter some illusions about a lot of people.'

Marcus had told stories against himself as much as amusing ones about some of his colleagues, and Joy had spent a couple of hilarious hours listening to him, her face still glowing with the enjoyment of it all. She had felt no hesitation at all in agreeing when Marcus had suggested they go back to her flat for coffee.

She felt slightly as if she was floating on air as she moved about her kitchen preparing a pot of coffee and knew that she owed that feeling as much to the euphoria of being in Marcus's company as she did to the wine they had consumed with their meal. Marcus had a way of making her feel good about herself, of filling her with an inner glow.

Marcus looked up from glancing through her book collection to smile at her warmly. 'I'm not sure that I really want coffee after that huge meal,' he said ruefully as he took the tray from her and placed it down on the table-top.

Joy looked up at him expectantly. And that was her undoing. As soon as their gazes met they both forgot about the coffee completely; both of them knew it had only been an excuse for them to be alone together in her flat, anyway.

'I enjoyed lunch, Joy,' Marcus told her gruffly as he moved slowly towards her.

Joy stood mesmerised by his gaze, the sheer animal magnetism of him. 'So did I,' she agreed.

'And I don't want to leave now,' he added huskily as he stood directly in front of her.

She didn't want him to leave either. It was as if the whole time they had been out for lunch had been leading up to this moment, the moment when they just melted into each other's arms.

And Joy did melt into Marcus's arms, her face raised as their lips met in no gentle exploratory kiss; the passion that had merely been simmering beneath the surface was instantly there between them.

It was as if no time had really elapsed since the last occasion they had been in each other's arms, as if they had only been biding their time until this moment.

'I want you so much, Joy,' Marcus murmured raggedly against her throat.

She wanted him too, ached with wanting him, knew she had done so for days now. And she didn't want to go on denying those feelings any longer. Now was now. Tomorrow could take care of itself.

She swallowed hard. 'I want you too,' she told him throatily.

He raised his head to look down at her, his dark blue gaze searching as he looked into her face flushed with desire, noting the slight apprehension there. 'There will be nothing to regret, Joy,' he assured her softly, his arms about her waist, moulding her body to his. 'I promise you.'

She didn't want to talk about regrets now, long-term or otherwise; she just wanted him. 'Take me to bed, Marcus,' she said almost pleadingly; she wanted him so badly that she was trembling with the emotion.

'Trust me,' he encouraged gruffly as he effortlessly swung her up into his arms. 'I would never hurt you, Joy,' he assured her as he paused outside her bedroom door.

Joy gazed up at him unblinkingly, aware of the enormity of what she was about to do. But she didn't care. She loved this man, wanted him to make love to her, wanted to make love to him. Surely that was all that mattered.

'I trust you, Marcus,' she said without hesitation; whatever happened between them in future, she didn't believe he would ever deliberately hurt her.

He gave a tortured sound in his throat, bending his head briefly to kiss her hard on the mouth. 'I've never met anyone like you before, Joy,' he groaned huskily.

And she had never met anyone like him before either.

And she loved him . . .

CHAPTER TEN

JOY woke slowly, her body aching slightly as she moved, but it was a pleasurable ache. Pleasurable? How could——

Her lids flew open, and she turned quickly to look at the man lying in the bed beside her. Marcus! And as she looked at him all the memories of the last few hours came rushing back.

Marcus had been a gentle but masterful lover, had raised her to the heights time and time again as they kissed and caressed each other's bodies. Joy quivered with delight as she recalled the hard beauty of Marcus's body, his muscular shoulders and chest, with their fine covering of dark hair, hair that went down over his flat stomach to the hard contours of his thighs, and down the long length of his legs.

And he had seemed to find her nakedness equally beautiful, telling her time after time how lovely she was as he kissed and touched each part of her.

Joy had never known such intimacy; she had burned with an ache deep inside her as he suckled her breasts, his hands gentle as they caressed the silky length of her body, more than ready for his as the hard sheath of his body finally claimed hers.

There had been little pain, Marcus having pleasured her to a pitch where even that slight discomfort didn't matter, her pleasure quickly building to a climax as Marcus moved slowly, and then much more quickly inside her.

It was the first time she had ever known such physical pleasure, and Joy had felt as if her body had soared high into space, her face full of disbelief at the all-consuming waves of ecstasy that washed over her.

That had been the first time, but Marcus had taken her to that plateau time and time again before finally joining her in a climax that rocked them both to their foundations. They had stared at each other in awe, Marcus's hands framing her face as he looked down at her with eyes that had appeared almost black.

Joy had returned that gaze almost shyly, incredulous at her own abandonment to passion, at knowing that Marcus had shared that passion to the ultimate.

And even afterwards, as she lay cradled in his arms, there had been none of the awkwardness or embarrassment she had expected the first time she made love with any man. There had been only tenderness, a feeling of being cocooned in the feelings they had evoked in each other; both of them had been sleepy, that sleepiness punctuated with tender kisses.

But they had finally fallen asleep, exhausted by their own need of each other. And Marcus still slept on, his face relaxed, almost boyish, completely vulnerable.

For long, lingering minutes Joy gazed upon the face of the man she loved, tentatively reaching out to touch one beard-darkened cheek, not wanting to disturb his sleep, but just needing the physical reassurance of touching him.

She loved him more than ever, felt as if she now belonged to him. Oh, God! The realisation of that terrified the life out of her. What if, now that they had become lovers, he no longer wanted her in his life, in any capacity? What would she do? How could she survive without this man?

The enormity of her disturbing thoughts brought her quickly out of the bed, taking care not to wake Marcus as she pulled on a robe and quietly left the bedroom.

What did she have to look forward to? A few months of an affair with Marcus? Possibly continuing on to the autumn, as Marcus was going to be in the area then anyway?

But it was a few months she hadn't expected to have, with a man she loved more than she had believed it possible to love anyone. It was more than a lot of people ever had in their lives, she reasoned to herself as she sat huddled in a chair, her knees drawn up to her chin. Time with Marcus, no matter how long it lasted, was more than she had ever hoped for herself. She would just have to make the best of it, enjoy every moment. Because she might have to live the rest of her life on those too-few memories . . .

And now was not the time to feel sad about that, she decided purposefully. There would be plenty of time later for sadness. Now she just wanted to live every moment to the full.

Her mind made up, she got up decisively, going through to the kitchen to make herself the cup of coffee they had foregone when they had arrived back. It was as she sat down again that she noticed the post she had picked up from the floor earlier and placed uninterestedly on the table; she hadn't been interested in anything but Marcus then.

She left the padded envelope until last, dealing with the usual array of circulars and bills first; the padded envelope was the only one that looked in the least interesting.

Although she wasn't quite so sure she wanted to open that when she saw the return address on the front of the envelope. It was from the magazine in which Casey had won the competition.

Glossy photographs of herself and Danny Eames fell out of the envelope into her lap, half a dozen in all, taken from different angles, some with the two of them smiling directly at each other, some with them smiling at the camera. But in all of them Joy noticed that her body was half turned towards Danny, the lack of a back to the dress she was wearing completely noticeable. Wonderful!

The last items to fall out of the envelope were two white sheets of paper, a compliments slip attached to the top of them, plus a large copy of one of the photographs, one in which she and Danny were smiling at each other in supposed total enjoyment of each other's company. As she read the brief note on the compliments slip, she realised that this was the photograph chosen to appear in the follow-up article in the magazine, and the two sheets of white paper held the details of the article itself.

Joy read these in horror. Where had they got such details of the evening from? Danny, obviously! he had left nothing out, not even the meeting with some of his fellow-actors. The background details on Joy herself were a bit sketchy, but then, she appreciated that she wasn't the one the readers would really be interested in.

As she stared down in dismay at the photographs and article the bedroom door opened, and Marcus came into the room. He had pulled on his trousers to cover his nakedness, although his chest remained bare. Joy felt the colour darken her cheeks as she vividly remembered touching the hardness of that chest, running her fingers lightly through the dark sprinkling of hair there.

Marcus returned her gaze darkly. 'You should have woken me,' he said softly.

She swallowed hard. 'You were sleeping so peacefully.'

He nodded, giving a rueful smile as he ran a hand through the dark thickness of his hair. 'We were both...very tired.'

Satiated, was the word, Joy inwardly acknowledged. They had made love for hours, long beautiful hours that she would never, ever, forget.

She gathered up the post in her arms. 'I'll make you a cup of coffee.' She stood up, feeling very awkward, wondering what they were going to say to each other.

'I... What's this?' Marcus said curiously as he bent down to pick up something that she had dropped on the floor as she stood up.

To Joy's dismay she saw that it was one of the photographs of Danny and herself, the enlarged copy of the one to be used in the article: Joy standing within the circle of Danny's arm, her body pressed lightly against his as she half turned towards him, Danny smiling down warmly into her upturned face.

Marcus's expression tightened as he looked down at the photograph, and Joy could only guess at the thoughts that must be shooting through his mind. The photograph on its own did look rather incriminating, but she had no intention of showing Marcus the magazine article too.

Marcus looked up at her slowly, his eyes narrowed. 'What's this?' he repeated, this time speculatively.

What indeed? she thought with an inward grimace. How was she going to explain away the photograph? 'I——' She was saved by the bell—literally—the doorbell, ringing at that precise moment, stopping her having to add anything further.

However, neither of them was exactly dressed to receive visitors—Joy wearing only her robe, and Marcus bare down to his waist.

Who could it be? It was eight-thirty at night, and—— Casey! It had to be Casey. She had been expecting to hear from him all day, after the four of them had had dinner together last night. And God knew what her cousin would make of Marcus being here again this evening.

'It will probably be Casey,' she warned.

'I'll go and put some more clothes on,' Marcus told her levelly, before going back into the bedroom.

And Joy noticed that he took the photograph with him. Damn! She was sure their conversation concerning that photograph was far from over.

She placed the rest of the mail out of the way in a drawer before going to answer the door; the last thing she wanted was for Marcus to come back into the sitting-room and see the rest of the photographs and the magazine article. It was going to be difficult enough explaining away that one photograph, without that.

Gerald was the one standing on her doorstep, admittedly looking rather sheepish, but he stood there nonetheless. 'You didn't call me,' he said, somewhat reproachfully.

She hadn't telephoned him because, at the time he had been expecting her to call, she had been in bed with Marcus. 'No,' she acknowledged lamely. 'I—I've been rather busy.' That had to be an understatement!

'I really do need to talk with you rather urgently, Joy.' He looked at her expectantly.

Joy had a feeling of sinking slowly into quicksands—and there wasn't a thing she could do about it. First the photograph of herself with Danny, and now this—were the fates totally against her?

She could put Gerald off again, of course she could; she owed him nothing. But somehow she knew it wasn't going to be as easy as that this time. Gerald had a slightly stubborn look about his mouth, and his stance was slightly defensive, as if he might put his foot in the doorway if she should try to close the door on him. God, this was awful. Much worse than the last couple of times he had turned up here uninvited.

'Doreen and I have decided to end our relationship,' he said encouragingly. 'Amicably,' he added quickly.

From the conversation Joy had had with him earlier, she doubted if the latter were true. And, from her own experience with him last year, she definitely doubted it even more. But Gerald seemed to have the ability to shut out anything he found too unpleasant, and delude himself into believing what he wanted to believe.

'Because of the feelings I still have for you,' Gerald continued earnestly as Joy still looked at him wordlessly.

What feelings he still had for her? Considering the abrupt way he had brought their own relationship to an end, Joy wasn't sure he had ever had any.

'Do we have a visitor?' drawled an all too familiar voice, and Joy turned sharply to find Marcus standing just behind her.

She had delayed too long in asking Gerald politely to go away. But, in truth, that quicksand feeling seemed to have rendered her immobile. She simply felt a sense of the inevitable.

'We?' Gerald repeated sharply as he glared at the other man. 'Joy?' he prompted abruptly.

'Why don't you come in?' Marcus invited smoothly. 'We were just about to make a pot of coffee,' he added, deftly removing Joy's hand from the door as he spoke, opening the door wider for the other man to enter.

Another 'we', Joy noted dazedly, staring uncomprehendingly at Marcus as he ushered the other man into her sitting-room before turning back to her expectantly. She followed the two men in a complete daze.

'How about that pot of coffee?' Marcus prompted softly. 'Or would you like me to make it?' he offered lightly.

As if he knew where anything was in her kitchen! Although she realised, by the look of displeasure

on Gerald's face, that he obviously believed the
other man did. As he was meant to. What game
was Marcus playing?

And if she didn't want to leave the two men
alone—something she definitely didn't want to do—
how was she to avoid adding to that impression?
The obvious answer was just to leave Marcus to his
own devices in her kitchen; he would quickly show
that he hadn't got a clue where anything was!

She gave him a bright, meaningless smile. 'That
would be lovely. Thank you.'

He turned to the other man. 'Coffee all right for
you, Gerald?' he said smoothly, further as-
tounding the confused Gerald by the fact that he
knew his name.

'Er—yes. Thank you,' Gerald answered him
dazedly.

Marcus nodded abruptly before going into the
kitchen—leaving a very awkward silence behind
him.

Joy looked at Gerald uncomfortably, very conscious of the accusation in his gaze. But what right
did he have to look at her like that? He had walked
out of her life six months ago, and hadn't cared
what had happened to her in the meantime; he certainly had no right to sit in judgement of her behaviour now, which she sensed he *was* doing.

Joy stood up abruptly. 'I think I'll go and put
some clothes on.'

'Just exactly what is going on between you and
Ballantyne, Joy?' Gerald could obviously hold back
his curiosity no longer.

She turned back to him with icy green eyes. 'I
don't think that's any——'

'Darling, where have you moved the sugar?' Marcus interrupted from the kitchen doorway, looking at her with a deceptively mild expression— deceptive because Joy could see the hard glitter in his eyes.

Joy was becoming agitated by this whole situation. It was difficult enough for Marcus and herself after what had happened between them this afternoon—at least, she felt it was—without Gerald's presence adding to the strain.

'It's where it usually is,' she returned abruptly. 'In the red bowl on the side,' she relented, as she saw the hardening of his mouth. She had no doubt that in any verbal fencing between Marcus and herself, with Gerald as their audience, she would be the loser.

Marcus shook his head. 'It doesn't appear to be.'

'I——'

'Perhaps you should just come and find it for me,' he suggested lightly, although the message in his eyes told her it was far from being a request— it was more like an order.

She gave an impatient sigh before preceding him into the kitchen, not in the least surprised when she saw the sugar-bowl sitting in plain view on the work-surface—or when Marcus firmly closed the door behind them both.

Marcus came up behind her and put his hands on her shoulders. 'I think you should go and put some clothes on, don't you?' he said, close to her ear-lobe. 'I'm sure Gerald has been a good friend in the past, but I don't think it's quite the thing now to sit and have coffee with him in your robe.'

Marcus was jealous! She knew it as surely as if he had said the words out loud. He really didn't like her being in her robe, she was sure, but he also didn't like her being alone in the sitting-room with the other man. How ridiculous—when it was her love for Marcus that had shown her how light-weight her emotions had been for Gerald. But she appreciated that Marcus couldn't know that. Probably never would. She could hardly express deep, abiding love for a man who only offered her an affair—an affair she had already allowed to begin!

She didn't attempt to turn and face Marcus. 'That's where I was going when you came and asked where the sugar-bowl was,' she told him, almost wearily.

'Good,' he said with satisfaction, turning her firmly to face him. 'I'll have the coffee ready by the time you come back.'

Joy didn't doubt that he would. Marcus might not be familiar with her kitchen, but he was capable enough of finding his way around.

She looked up at him, wondering exactly where this day was going to end. He was her lover, and she loved him, but how did he feel about her?

'Don't be long,' he murmured softly as he bent his head and kissed her lingeringly on the lips. 'I'll miss you.'

Joy passed through the sitting-room without even looking at Gerald, so dazed was she by Marcus's last remark. Of course, he could have said that just to achieve this effect, but he had never used sub-terfuge with her before; he had always been direct with her, embarrassingly so on occasions, so she didn't have any reason to disbelieve him this time, either.

She wished Gerald would leave so that she and Marcus could talk. Really talk. Because she realised that they couldn't go on as they had been; Marcus might have been truthful with her, but she was well aware that she had been far from honest with him—self-protectively so, but, nevertheless, she hadn't been completely honest with him. And it was time all that changed.

She dressed distractedly, putting on denims and a loose navy-blue blouse tucked in at her narrow waist, brushing her hair until it fell in glistening waves down her back, the high colour in her cheeks making make-up unnecessary.

Marcus did indeed have the coffee ready by the time Joy rejoined the two men in the sitting-room. Marcus was listening interestedly; he seemed to have got the other man talking about the library.

Both men turned in her direction as she came into the room. Gerald was sitting in one of the armchairs, Marcus to one side on the sofa. Joy hesitated as she crossed the room.

Marcus sat forward slightly. 'I've put the tray here for you so you can pour the coffee.' He indicated the low table in front of the sofa, really telling her that he expected her to sit next to him. 'I'm sure you know how we both take our coffee,' he added, his expression deceptively innocent as Joy looked at him sharply.

Of course she knew how Gerald took his coffee, and she had realised at dinner the night before that Marcus took his black and unsweetened. She made no reply to the provocative remark as she sat down to pour the coffee, wordlessly handing the two men their steaming cups.

Gerald, despite Marcus's effort to put him at his ease by getting him to talk about his work, looked very uncomfortable about this whole situation, his brow furrowed as he stared across the table at Joy.

What did he expect of her? Just exactly what did he want? She was becoming as exasperated by the situation as he appeared to be.

'So you're Joy's boss.' Marcus was finally the one to break the awkward silence that seemed to have fallen since Joy came back into the room.

Gerald's frown deepened. 'I was also Joy's fiancé,' he rasped harshly.

Joy gasped, her eyes wide as she stared at him. They might have gone out together for four years, and after that length of time Joy might have expected that he would one day propose to her, but, as far as she was aware, they had never actually been engaged to each other.

'And I would like to be again,' he added, sitting forward tensely as he met Joy's even more astounded gaze.

This was awful. What on earth was Gerald doing? He had put her, and himself, in a very difficult position by saying this in front of Marcus. Because, alone or in front of an audience, her reply to this statement had to be a very firm no.

'I'm afraid that won't be possible.' Marcus was the one to break quietly into the strained silence that had ensued after Gerald's announcement, and both Joy and Gerald looked at him now, instead of at each other. 'Because Joy is going to marry me,' he announced arrogantly, taking a firm hold of one of her hands as it rested on the sofa beside him, his fingers entwining with hers, preventing escape.

Not that she wanted to escape, or, indeed, had the strength to do so. Not only had she had a long-awaited proposal of marriage from Gerald, but now Marcus was making the same claim.

Her head was spinning, her thoughts in turmoil. Was Marcus serious? Surely he couldn't be?

'Joy, is this true?' Gerald burst out indignantly.

How did she know? Until a few seconds ago it had been something she had not dared, even in her wildest dreams, to think about!

'Of course it's true.' Again Marcus was the one to answer the other man, his grip still tight on Joy's hand. 'I'm staying here at the moment so that we can sort out the wedding arrangements.'

Was he? Surely it was an affair he had been suggesting, not marriage? Joy just didn't know any more, was totally confused by everything at this moment.

'Joy?' Gerald looked at her with those accusing eyes again.

Marcus's fingers squeezed hers warningly, although to outward appearances he sat quite confidently at her side, not even glancing her way.

Joy had no idea whether Marcus really wanted to marry her or not—but she did know that she had no intention of accepting Gerald's proposal; she never would have been able to after meeting Marcus.

'It's true, Gerald.' She was amazed at how calmly controlled her voice sounded. She had expected to sound like a quivering wreck—which was exactly how she felt. Now she just wanted Gerald to leave, so that she and Marcus could talk privately. 'We'll send you an invitation,' she added distractedly.

He looked totally outraged. 'Are you sure you're doing the right thing, Joy? After all——' he shot Marcus a scathing glance '—you hardly know the man!'

On the surface that might appear to be true, but she had thought she knew Gerald, and look how disastrously that had turned out. The important thing for her to know about Marcus was that she loved him.

'I hardly think that's relevant, Gerald,' Marcus drawled dismissively. 'Sometimes it just happens this way.' He shrugged.

'But——'

'Joy and I are going to be married, Gerald,' Marcus cut in firmly, seeming unaware of the way the other man almost winced every time he called him by his name. 'It isn't a subject that's open for discussion.' He looked at the older man challengingly.

Gerald met that gaze for several tension-filled seconds, and then his own gaze dropped away. 'Then there's nothing more to be said, is there?' he finally said tightly.

'Absolutely nothing,' Marcus acknowledged lightly.

Gerald stood up abruptly, looking down at Joy. 'I hope you aren't making a mistake,' he bit out tautly.

Marcus stood up too. 'I'll see you to the door.'

Joy seemed incapable of moving. She was still stunned by Marcus's announcement, and couldn't have stood up to walk over to the door with Gerald even if she had wanted to.

'I'm not sure we were exactly kind to him,' Marcus said regretfully as he came back from seeing the other man out. 'But, considering his arrogance, I'm not sure he deserved for us to be kind to him,' he added. 'Joy?' He looked down at her frowningly as she made no response. 'Did you want to marry him?'

Of course she didn't want to marry Gerald; she wanted to marry Marcus. But she wasn't sure if he was serious about his announcement, or if it had just been a way to get rid of Gerald. If it was the latter, then it had been a bit drastic.

'No,' she answered slowly. 'I thought I did once, but he went off with someone else.' There, it was said. Now he knew that Gerald had considered someone else more attractive than she was.

'The man obviously has no taste,' Marcus returned grimly. 'But he's now decided he wants you back,' he added harshly.

'So it would appear,' she acknowledged, wondering how much of Gerald's behaviour was due to that 'dog-in-the-manger' tendency that Casey had once spoken of in Gerald.

'You're well rid of him, Joy.' Marcus looked at her intently.

'I believe so.' She nodded, still looking across at Marcus.

His eyes were narrowed. 'How long did you go out with him?'

She shrugged. 'Four years.'

'Four years!' he repeated, obviously astounded. 'And you and he never—— What does the man have in his veins, ice-water?' he said disgustedly.

Marcus *knew*. Despite the fact that there had only been the briefest moment of discomfort, Marcus knew she had been a virgin when they had made love this afternoon. Was that why he had made that announcement about the two of them getting married? Did he feel——?

'What are you thinking now, Joy?' Marcus moved to kneel down on the carpet next to where she still sat on the sofa, his hands clasping hers as they rested in her lap. 'Joy, this afternoon you gave me the biggest gift any woman can ever give a man,' he told her gently, his gaze caressing her flushed face. 'Besides her love, of course.' His gaze was intent now.

She loved him. Of course she loved him. That had been the gift she gave him this afternoon.

'I love you, Joy,' he said huskily, his hands tightening briefly on hers. 'I want to marry you. Will you be my wife?'

She swallowed hard. 'You don't know me——'

'Of course I know you,' he cut in with firm dismissal. 'If you're talking about all the details of your life, your childhood, family, friends, then, no, I don't know those things about you yet. But we can have a lifetime together to discover those things about each other. Because I do know *you*, Joy,' he added intently. 'I knew you the moment I first saw you in that restaurant with Danny. You're the woman I love.'

Joy looked searchingly into his face, at the clear certainty of his love glowing in his eyes. He *did* love her!

'Oh, Marcus!' she cried emotionally, throwing herself into the warm safety of his arms. 'I love you too. I love you so very much!'

He held her tightly against him, her head cradled against his shoulder as they both sat now on the carpeted floor. 'I hoped you did,' he groaned huskily. 'This afternoon, when I realised... I hoped to God you loved me—because there's no way I could let you walk away from my life now. *Will* you marry me, Joy?' Once again he looked down into her flushed face.

'Oh, yes!' she agreed, without hesitation. There was no way she couldn't marry him, not now that she knew how he felt about her too. 'But will I fit into your world, Marcus?' She frowned her doubts. 'I'm not——'

'"My world", as you put it, will fit in around you,' he assured her decisively. 'We can travel together. And once we have children we can organise my career around——'

'Children?' she repeated breathlessly. 'Will we have children, Marcus?' She could already see a little boy, an exact replica of his father; the very thought of that was exhilarating.

Marcus frowned down at her. 'Not if you don't want them. It's just that you're such a warm woman, so caring, I assumed... Maybe I shouldn't have assumed.' He shook his head. 'If you don't want children——'

'Of course I want children,' she laughingly interrupted him, cradling his face lovingly. 'Your children!'

There was silence, apart from their loving murmurings, for a long time after this announcement.

Joy lay in the strength of Marcus's arms, her head resting on his shoulder, the wild blaze of her hair fanned out over his arm. She had never been so happy; she felt as if she might burst with the feelings of love inside her.

Marcus looked down ruefully at their nakedness. 'Is either Casey or Danny likely to come knocking on your door?' he teased. 'Because, if so, I suggest we don't answer!'

Joy frowned slightly. 'About Danny——'

'You don't have to tell me about him, if you don't want to,' Marcus reassured her lightly. 'I know what I need to know; it's me you love.'

She shook her head. 'Let me show you something, then you'll understand.' She stood up to cross the room to the drawer where she had put the envelope that had arrived from the magazine, unashamedly naked, knowing from the hours she had spent in Marcus's arms that he found her beautiful. As she did him. She wordlessly handed him the envelope. 'I didn't want to tell you before——' she grimaced as he began to read the article '— because I felt embarrassed about the whole thing. Casey won this competition, you see, and——'

'I think I can guess the rest,' Marcus nodded, putting the article to one side to take her back into his arms.

Joy looked up at him anxiously. 'Can you?'

'Knowing Casey, as I have come to, yes!' He nodded. 'You can fill me in on the details another time. All that's really relevant about that week is that the two of us managed to meet. Although it does explain the confusion over the name Casey,' he added teasingly. 'An old family name, indeed!' he chided mockingly.

Joy relaxed again, knowing that what had seemed like a complete disaster was actually unimportant to Marcus. And he was right. If she hadn't gone for that week to London, the two of them would never have met...

'So you didn't even know Danny until that evening,' Marcus mused lightly.

'No.' She made a face. 'And I quickly decided I never wanted to see him again after it either.'

'But he made you feel responsible for his dismissal from *Pilgrim's Game*,' Marcus guessed knowingly. 'That was a production decision, Joy,' he added seriously. 'Danny Eames has been a thorn in the side of the production since the series first began, has cost the company thousands.'

'You really don't have to tell me any of this.' She knew Marcus well enough now to know that he would never have been unfair in his decision.

'Yes, I do,' he said firmly. 'It's as well if it's out of the way and forgotten about. I can guess at the things you've been thinking about that situation. But the competition Casey entered is a prime example of Danny's behaviour.' He frowned. 'Danny's contract states that he has to OK all publicity through the production company, but he's been going his own way for months now, arrogantly doing whatever he damn well feels like. I know there's a saying that any publicity is better than none, but, nevertheless, there is a policy, and it's clearly written into the contract Danny was only too eager to sign at the time.'

And Joy now realised that Danny's reasons for not wanting Marcus to know about the competition that evening were more to do with the fact that he was breaking his contract than with his male ego not wanting Marcus to know that he had been the prize in a competition.

She frowned. 'But surely he realised you would find out about it at some time—that there would be the article in the magazine, for one thing?'

'Of course.' Marcus nodded grimly. 'But presenting the company with a *fait accompli* puts us in a very awkward position. He was warned time and time again, and I'm afraid that day he disrupted shooting was the one time too many.' He shook his head. 'Some people never learn. And I'm afraid Danny Eames is one of them.'

'But isn't it difficult just to sack him?' Joy said thoughtfully. 'After all, he is your partner in the programme.'

'Plans to write that particular character out of the programme have been going on for some time.' Marcus sighed. 'But, hopefully, it's going to be done in such a way that it adds to the programme, not detracts from it. Danny, unfortunately, is going to learn the hard way that you are only as good as your last appearance. And I accidentally shoot his character in the final episode of this series.'

Hence Marcus being responsible for Danny's 'demise'!

'Don't worry.' Marcus's arms tightened about her. 'He won't be out of work for long. In fact, once it's been brought home to him that no one is irreplaceable, I'm considering offering him the lead in the play I'm directing,' he told her ruefully.

Joy looked at him incredulously. 'Is that wise?'

He laughed softly. 'Who knows? But he's a talented actor. He just needs to learn some self-discipline—and consideration for his fellow-actors. Hopefully, losing *Pilgrim's Game* might do that. We'll see,' he added dismissively.

Joy didn't doubt that Marcus was more than capable of handling the situation—more than capable of handling Danny.

And he was in love with her.

As she was in love with him.

'Marcus, I——' She broke off as the doorbell rang. 'This time it *has* to be Casey,' she said with a rueful grimace, slowly rising to her feet.

'Good.' Marcus nodded his satisfaction as he pulled on his clothes. 'Because we're going to need a best man for the wedding.'

Joy was filled with a happy glow as she quickly picked up her clothes to go into the bedroom and dress while Marcus went to answer the door.

The wedding.

She was going to marry Marcus.

It was a dream come true.

'Will you stop worrying, Joy?' Casey soothed, holding her hand tightly. 'Marcus has promised to be here, so he will be,' he said with certainty.

'But it's the first night of the play opening in the West End!' Joy wailed in distress.

'It's also the night his son or daughter is about to be born,' Lisa chided as she sat at Casey's side. 'I know which Marcus considers the most important.'

The last year had been one of the happiest Joy could ever have imagined. She and Marcus had become a partnership, not only in their marriage, but also in Marcus's work. Joy went everywhere with the man she loved, and who obviously loved her deeply in return, and had become his assistant, once she knew what was required of her.

And now she was about to give birth to their first child.

She hadn't been able to believe it was actually labour when the pains started late this afternoon; the baby wasn't due for another three weeks. But as the afternoon and early evening progressed, the pains becoming stronger with the passing of time, she had had to acknowledge that she *was* actually in labour, that their child wasn't about to wait any longer to make its début into the world.

But Marcus had worked long and hard for the opening tonight, and so it had been Casey and Lisa she had rung to drive her to the hospital, not alerting Marcus at the theatre until Casey had insisted they do so, the doctor having informed him that the birth was imminent.

The labour pains were incredible, unlike anything Joy had ever imagined, and she was sure she must have done irreparable damage to Casey's hand as she squeezed hard on his fingers every time a contraction hit her. But, now that she knew Marcus was on his way, she had no intention of this baby being born before he arrived.

But when he burst through the doorway of the labour-room a few minutes later, his eyes dark with worry, she knew a sudden calm, instantly knowing that everything was going to be all right now. Marcus was here. That was all that mattered.

'The cavalry!' Casey grinned as he stood up to let Marcus take his place, and he and Lisa quietly left the room.

Marcus sat down next to Joy, taking one of her hands in his, smoothing back the dampness of her hair with his other hand.

'How is the play going?' She looked up at him.

'Never mind the damned play—Danny's giving the performance of a lifetime,' he relented as he saw the reproach in her eyes. 'But *you*, young lady, should have called me earlier. Should have——'

'I don't think we have time for this now, Mr Ballantyne,' the doctor told him lightly. 'Your son or daughter is about to make an entrance into the world.'

And, with that one final all-consuming pain, the doctor was right. Joy and Marcus were both laughing and crying at the same time as they heard the wail of their child as it entered the world.

'You have a beautiful daughter,' the doctor informed them seconds later, laying the squirming bundle on Joy's breast.

She was beautiful. Soft and silky, with skin like magnolia, and smooth red hair, her eyes dark blue as she opened them for the first time.

'Our Valentine,' Marcus said emotionally, gently touching one tightly clenched fist.

Joy looked at him curiously. They had discussed names for the baby, of course they had, but Valentine hadn't been one of them.

'We met on Valentine's night,' Marcus pointed out huskily, his eyes glowing with love for them both, a love Joy had never doubted during their year of marriage. 'Now it seems only fitting we should name our daughter after the night we met.'

He was so right, Joy realised. So very right.

Their Valentine.

BRIDE'S BAY RESORT

UNLOCK THE DOOR TO GREAT ROMANCE AT BRIDE'S BAY RESORT

Join Harlequin's new across-the-lines series, set in an exclusive hotel on an island off the coast of South Carolina.

Seven of your favorite authors will bring you exciting stories about fascinating heroes and heroines discovering love at Bride's Bay Resort.

Look for these fabulous stories coming to a store near you beginning in January 1996.

Harlequin American Romance #613 in January
Matchmaking Baby by Cathy Gillen Thacker

Harlequin Presents #1794 in February
Indiscretions by Robyn Donald

Harlequin Intrigue #362 in March
Love and Lies by Dawn Stewardson

Harlequin Romance #3404 in April
Make Believe Engagement by Day Leclaire

Harlequin Temptation #588 in May
Stranger in the Night by Roseanne Williams

Harlequin Superromance #695 in June
Married to a Stranger by Connie Bennett

Harlequin Historicals #324 in July
Dulcie's Gift by Ruth Langan

Visit Bride's Bay Resort each month wherever Harlequin books are sold.

HARLEQUIN ®

YOUR SPECIAL KISS!

This Valentine's Day, Harlequin and Silhouette have a very special offer for you!

Are you impetuous, impulsive, flirtatious, racy?

Your lip print can reveal all! Just send an imprint of your lips (on the special ad found in this book) and Harlequin and Silhouette will send you an analysis, detailing what secrets your lips can tell. And as an added bonus, just for participating, you can receive a free Coty '24' lipstick. (A $5.75 Retail value).

Coty '24' lipstick won't feather, fade or even budge. Long-wearing, Coty '24' will ensure your lips always look their best—hour after hour, time after time!

With Coty '24' lipstick, you will always have

A LASTING KISS!

YOUR SPECIAL KISS!

Are your lips succulent, impetuous, delicious or racy?

Find out just how *special* your kiss can be!
Put your lip print in the box below, send it
to Harlequin® and we will send you a free
lip analysis, plus as an added FREE bonus,
a Coty '24'* lipstick—for lips that won't quit!
(A $5.75 Retail value).

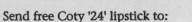

Please send me the following lipstick color:
☐ Rose
☐ Amber

Send free Coty '24' lipstick to:

Name:_____

Address: _____

City: _____ State/Prov.: _____ Zip/Postal Code:_____

Put lip print in box below:

```
┌─────────────────────────────────────┐
│                                     │
│                                     │
│                                     │
│                                     │
│                                     │
└─────────────────────────────────────┘
```

Return lip print, name and address,
plus $1.25 in the U.S., $2.25 in Canada
for postage and handling, to:

In the U.S.	**In Canada**
Harlequin Your Special Kiss Promotion	Harlequin Your Special Kiss Promotion
P.O. Box 1387	P.O. Box 609
Buffalo, NY 14240-1387	Fort Erie, ONT. L2A 5X3

Please allow 4-6 weeks for delivery.

*Coty '24' is a registered trademark of Coty, Inc.

VALLIP

Yo amo novelas con corazón!

Starting this March, Harlequin opens up to a whole new world of readers with two new romance lines in SPANISH!

Harlequin Deseo
- passionate, sensual and exciting stories

Harlequin Bianca
- romances that are fun, fresh and very contemporary

With four titles a month, each line will offer the same wonderfully romantic stories that you've come to love—now available in Spanish.

Look for them at selected retail outlets.

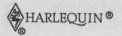 HARLEQUIN®

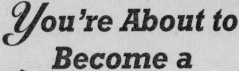

You're About to Become a Privileged Woman

Reap the rewards of fabulous free gifts and benefits with proofs-of-purchase from Harlequin and Silhouette books

Pages & Privileges™

It's our way of thanking you for buying our books at your favorite retail stores.

PROOF OF PURCHASE
HP-PP104
Offer expires October 31, 1996

Harlequin and Silhouette—
the most privileged readers in the world!

For more information about Harlequin and Silhouette's PAGES & PRIVILEGES program call the Pages & Privileges Benefits Desk: 1-503-794-2499

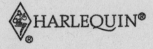

HARLEQUIN®

HP-PP104